The Irishman's Christmas Gamble

A Wager of Hearts Novella

Nancy Herkness

Praise for the Novels of Nancy Herkness

"Be it an emotional moment or an erotic encounter, Nancy has the ability to tie your emotions and heart-strings in knots."

—Karen Laird, *Shade Book Tree Reviews*

"Herkness always brings a refreshing, riveting mix of personality, passion and complications to the table."

—Kathy Altman, *USA Today HEA*

"Bestseller Herkness shines with…catchy dialogue, memorable characters, and top-notch writing."

—*Publishers Weekly* Starred Review

CHAPTER ONE

"Ms. Hogan, there's a gentleman waiting to see you in the reception area."

Frankie raised her eyebrows at Vincent, her head of security, as she stepped out of the elevator from her penthouse apartment in the Bellwether Club. "I don't have an appointment this afternoon," she said, surprised that her protective staff members would let an unknown, non-member into her ultra-exclusive club.

"Donal vouched for him."

Frankie's curiosity stirred. Her head bartender wouldn't override her head of security without a damned compelling reason. She strode across the hallway and into the waiting room. It was empty, which meant the mystery man had entered her office without permission.

She stalked through the door to see the silhouette of a man standing with his back to her as he gazed through the French doors at the snow-covered garden.

"My office is private," she snapped. "You may enter it only at my invitation."

"That's not the greeting I had hoped for."

Shock crackled through her, making her stomach flutter with nerves. She knew that dark voice with the lilt of Ireland flowing in it. It rippled through her like a tide, sucking her back into places she didn't want to go.

"Liam," she whispered.

Sun-glare from the snow dazzled Frankie's vision, so even though Liam turned, she couldn't see his face. But she recognized the coiled energy of his athlete's body, ready to explode in whatever direction the football—no, in her adopted country, it was a soccer ball—flew. But he was broader now, his muscles filled out and solid, rather than lean and ropey like a boy's. The flutters in her stomach settled and warmed and moved lower, setting off sensations inside her that she'd forgotten she'd ever felt.

"Good to know you recognize an old friend," he said.

"I couldn't see you against the light from outside," she said, forcing her voice to remain normal.

He glanced toward the window, and she saw the strong lines of his profile limned against the light. His blade of a nose with the bump partway down the bridge from the break he'd gotten when he'd come to her rescue in a dirty Dublin alley. The clean jut of his chin, signaling the determination that had hauled him out of the slums of their childhood and into international glory as Arsenal's star center midfielder.

"I was admiring your view." He started around the desk with that long-legged grace that sent a shudder of remembered desire through her.

His movement seemed to unlock her muscles so that she could take a step toward him, her hands held out in affectionate greeting, as though she didn't want to hurl herself into his arms. "Sure, and it's good to see you, Liam," she said, letting the full Irish into her voice.

She had only a brief glimpse of his face before he took her hands and drew her against the warm, solid wall of his chest, wrapping his arms like iron bands around her back. "*A stór*," he said, his voice husky.

My treasure. He'd called her that the day he'd left for the football…soccer academy in England. The day he'd kissed her with all the frustrated arousal in his 18-year-old body. Her 26-year-old body had answered with a leap of ecstasy, as his big, powerful hands roamed over her back and his hot, firm lips slanted against hers. She'd yearned to give in to the pleasures of his beautiful muscles and sinews, wanted to feel his skin slide naked against hers. But he was still a boy in years, if not experience. And they both had grand plans, without any room for love in them.

Yet she felt the same searing hunger now, the liquid desire spreading when he shifted against her. More than two decades evaporated as she pressed against the hard, curving muscles beneath the layers of suit and shirt. "Prince," she breathed the nickname she'd given him for his pride. The neighborhood kids had picked it up because it suited him so well.

She felt a shiver run through him. "No one's called me that in years," he said.

She turned her cheek to rest against him for just a second more, inhaling the scent of clean cotton and warm male and hearing the deep, even rhythm of his heartbeat. Then she wedged her hands between them and pushed until he released her.

She stepped back and looked up, bracing herself for the slash of his high cheekbones, the deep auburn of his waving hair, the dark blue burn of his gaze. She forced her voice to remain level. "Are you in New York to meet your new team?"

Disappointment flickered in his eyes. "Aye. And to inspect the facility. There are some changes that need to be made. I'm looking at apartments as well since I'll be settling here now." He surveyed her. "You look grand, Frankie. Beautiful."

She looked as she did every day, dressed in her usual uniform of a pantsuit custom-tailored for her short figure, her silver hair smoothed into a conservative pageboy style. Today's suit was dark red in a nod to the holiday season. She smiled a careful smile to hide the flush of pleasure that surged through her. "You look more like a king than a prince now. As befits the new head coach of the New York Challenge."

His smile deepened the lines etched around his mouth and at the corners of his eyes. "As befits an old man in the world of soccer. I'm learning to call it that instead of football."

"You're only forty-one. That seems young to me."

The smile vanished. "So we're back to that again."

"Unless you've found a way to warp time," Frankie said. She didn't pretend to misunderstand. One of the reasons she'd pushed him away over and over again in their youth was that she was eight years his elder. Of course, she'd felt about a century older in experience, despite the fact that he lived in the same slum neighborhood she did. But he didn't have a drunkard for a father nor did he have seven younger siblings to take care of. For all that Liam's mother, Kathleen, complained that his father had bolted so she had to raise her son alone, Frankie thought Kathleen was lucky in her solitude.

Pushing the ugly memories away, she moved to the sleek, built-in bar. "Would you like a drink?"

"Would you be havin' some good Irish whiskey?"

"Redbreast 21," she said, setting out two cut-crystal tumblers and splashing the golden whiskey into them.

She handed him one glass. "Here's to the future," he said, holding her gaze as he touched his glass to hers with a musical clink.

Her chest went hollow as she recognized the toast they always drank while they plotted their paths away from their dismal beginnings. Away from each other.

"We made it out, Liam," she said, savoring the warmth of the spicy, single-pot still liquor. "We made a damned good future."

"It could be better." He tossed back the whole drink. "Have dinner with me tonight. We can catch up on the twenty-three years since we last saw each other." There was that edge in his voice again.

She should say no, partly just to douse his assumption that she would be available on such short notice. "Seven-thirty," she said. "We can use the private dining room here at the club."

"No, Frankie, I'm going to treat you, just like I promised back then. We're going to the most expensive restaurant in New York City. I'll pick you up at seven." He leaned down to brush a kiss across her lips, the gossamer touch igniting the blood in her veins again. "*A stór.*"

And he was gone.

Frankie sank into the nearest chair, staring out at the sinuous snow-dusted curves of the modern sculpture in her garden. Trying to separate the memory of Liam from the reality of him.

All the photographs she'd collected as his athletic career skyrocketed hadn't prepared her for the way his youthful arrogance had transformed into a confidence that he wore like a second skin. He moved as though the world would get out of his way.

And he'd reduced her to a hungry young girl again.

She hated that.

CHAPTER TWO

Liam jogged up the stone steps of the Bellwether Club. At least this time he didn't have to call his old friend Donal to get him through the well-guarded portal adorned with lush pine wreaths. The door swung open as he reached the portico, revealing a lean man dressed in a dark suit. He had the cold, blank stare of one of the thugs from the old neighborhood in Dublin.

"Welcome, Mr. Keller," the man said, in an entirely American accent. "I'll take you to Ms. Hogan's office."

It was intimidating, the Bellwether Club. Not because he hadn't been in plenty of other grand places with miles of mahogany paneling and fancy Oriental rugs, but because his old pal Frankie had created it, paid for it with her own money. It reminded him all too vividly that even the enormous sum of money his agent had wrung out of the mad

Americans was peanuts compared to Frankie's fortune. Which was going to make his task that much harder.

His cold-eyed escort gestured him through the door into the waiting room outside her office. She was standing by the garland-draped fireplace, staring into the flames. The firelight turned her silver hair to molten gold and sent light and shadows flickering across the sharp, clean lines of her face. Her beauty was achingly familiar, yet the years had changed it in subtle ways. As a girl, she had burned like a wild, blazing torch. Now her intensity was as sharp as a cutting laser.

Yet when she turned, warmth lit her gray eyes. "Liam," she said. "I can't quite get used to the sight of you. It's like seeing a ghost."

"Then let me convince you that I'm flesh and blood," he said, moving quickly to place a kiss on her soft lips, the contact brief but firm.

There was a tiny hitch in her voice as she said, "Proof positive you're human."

"And you as well. Not just a dream anymore." He let his eyes skim down the simple black dress she wore that hinted at dangerous curves underneath. She'd always had gorgeous legs and that hadn't changed. All the boys in their slum neighborhood of Finglas had wanted her, drawn to her fiery brilliance like moths to a flame. But she would have nothing to do with any of them.

Except for him. Because his plans were almost as big as hers. She'd shown him how to use his raw talent to leave the burnt-out cars and graffiti-scarred walls far behind. She'd researched which soccer leagues attracted the scouts from the English clubs and pushed him into them. When he needed to practice extra hours, she'd done his schoolwork for him. In the glorious moment when the Arsenal Academy had recruited him, she'd filled out the scholarship forms. Finally, she'd forced his mother to give her blessing to his departure, although he'd only discovered that years later.

Yet Frankie had refused to be anything more than his friend.

He brought his gaze back to her face, looking for a reaction to his blatantly appreciative survey, but she had her guard up now. She wasn't going to be surprised into letting him hold her in his arms again. When she had laid her cheek against his chest for that brief, stunning moment, his heart had stopped. It was more than he had expected, less than he had hoped for.

She reached for the coat draped over a chair by the fire, but he swept it up first, holding it so that he had an excuse to brush his fingers against the nape of her neck and feel the silk of her hair on the back of his hands.

"Your reflexes haven't slowed," she said as she picked up her purse.

"On the soccer pitch they have. That's why I've been coaching these last five years."

"Was it hard to stop playing?" Her gaze was locked on his face.

"The hardest thing I've ever done but for one." He knew he could play soccer. But when he retired, he'd had no idea if he could lead a team from the sidelines. "Was it hard to sell your company?"

"It was my goal from the day I started it." She headed for the door.

"That doesn't answer my question."

She stopped, her back to him. "I had no idea what to do after I signed the contract."

"They didn't have you stay on for the transition?"

"I told them I wouldn't." She pivoted back to him. "Can you imagine me taking orders from an outsider who knows less about the business than I do?"

"I thought you might have mellowed over the years."

But of course she hadn't. Even when she was young, she'd been tougher than the boys who followed her around like panting dogs. Thank God they did because when she'd been dragged into an alley by a drug dealer, a knife to her throat, one of the boys had seen the grab. The lad had run to tell Liam, thank Mary and Jesus. He'd sprinted as though he was trying out for Team Ireland, and hauled the thug off Frankie before her attacker had been able to pry her naked and bruised thighs apart.

The memory of her curled into a ball on the filthy cement littered with broken glass still made his gut clench. She hadn't cried. She just lay there as he tore the tee shirt off his back and draped it over the shreds of her clothing, begging her to tell him where she was hurt.

It wasn't until the blood from his broken nose dripped onto her cheek that she stirred. "You're bleeding. We need to get you taken care of." She had sat up and pulled his shirt on over her head as though it was an everyday occurrence. Taking his hand to rise to her feet, she looked him in the eye and said, "Thank you for saving me from my own stupidity. I'll never let happiness make me careless again."

He still didn't know what good fortune had made her forget her dangerous surroundings.

As the big limo glided to a stop, Frankie tried to peer out the window to see what restaurant Liam had chosen, but he flung open the door and leapt out before she had a chance.

On the ride to dinner, she'd been too focused on the man seated beside her to track their progress through the city. Being closed into the dark, private space with her oldest friend had brought back a rush of feelings and memories she had a hard time swimming through. It also brought a physical awareness that had her noticing every shift of his weight on the leather seat, every brush of his shoulder against hers, every rise and fall of his rumbling voice.

When he'd walked into her office in his dark, well-tailored suit, his auburn hair and blue eyes catching glints of firelight while shadows emphasized the hard angles of his face, she'd felt the pull of him low in her gut, not as a friend but as a powerful, sexual man.

He was Liam and not Liam. She would fall into a relaxed camaraderie with him and then he would say something to remind her that he had worked at an elite level on the international sports stage for many years. It unbalanced their old relationship where she was the wise, experienced mentor and he the eager, young follower.

The first time she'd seen Liam playing on the mudhole that passed for a local soccer pitch, he'd made every other player look like they were moving in slow motion. But it had been the desire and drive he telegraphed in every pass, every fake, every kick that snagged her attention. He burned with the passion to win. That was the moment she decided she would do everything in her power to get this brilliant kid out of the pit of despair that was Finglas. Maybe she wouldn't make it, but *he* would.

"Where are we?" Frankie said, setting her high heels on a gritty cement sidewalk and allowing Liam to help her out of the car. A curved stone wall rose up beside them and she tilted her head back to look up at it. The shape and texture were familiar but she had no way to orient herself after her inattention during the drive.

"The most expensive restaurant in New York City." His smile flashed white in the streetlights. "This is the private entrance to the Owner's Box in Yankee Stadium."

Frankie laughed. "You always could surprise me."

"When no one else could."

She didn't want to feel this bubble of delight expanding in her chest. "Don't you have to own the Yankees to eat here?"

"Or you can work for the owners, like I do." He held out his elbow and she put her hand through it. "In the off-season, they were willing to allow their newest hire to borrow it."

He led her toward a polished steel door with the New York Yankees logo set into the sidewalk in front of it. It opened at their approach, held by a balding man in a blue coverall. They walked to an elevator where the door keeper inserted a key and sent them soaring upwards.

The elevator opened onto a hallway with walls covered in blue suede and a floor paved with speckled granite. Liam led her to a double set of steel-and-glass doors. On each hung a wreath of entwined holly and ivy, adorned with a red velvet bow.

She slid a quick glance toward Liam. The holly and ivy were an Irish tradition, but were also not uncommon in her adopted country. He met her eyes but said nothing.

Pushing open the door, he bowed her through into a foyer before hanging her coat in the closet. When she stepped into the next room, Frankie gasped. Dozens of candles were lined up along the counter in front of the huge plate glass windows that formed one wall of the owner's box, their flames casting a flickering golden light.

"Mary and Joseph candles," Frankie whispered, her throat too clogged with tears to say it any louder. "To light their way to the stable on Christmas Eve."

"I saved one for you, even though it's not Christmas Eve." He brought her to an unlit candle at the end of the counter. The tall pillar of white wax was a foot tall and at least three inches in diameter, with raised golden angels molded into its sides. He picked up a long, fireplace match from the counter and handed it to her. "I figured because you were the eldest daughter in your family, you never got to light the candle."

As she took the match, memory yanked her back to the day the priest had given her a half-burnt church candle to place in the window of their flat on Christmas Eve. They didn't have the money to spend on useless decorations, so this was a magical gift. But tradition held that the youngest daughter was given the task of lighting the beacon for the weary travelers seeking an inn. Frankie was ten years old, with three younger sisters by then. She'd watched in envy as five-year-old Shauna's face had been illuminated by the glow of the flame when she kindled it to life.

Suddenly, tears painted warm tracks down Frankie's cheeks. She tried to hold the tip of the match to the nearest candle flame, but her hand shook. Liam took the match from her, his long fingers brushing hers. "I didn't expect this to upset you," he said, his voice tight with concern.

"Not upset, touched." She wiped at the wet streaks with the back of her hand. She'd never told Liam that story, just as she'd never told him so many of the squalid secrets of her family life. Yet he'd seen her gaze longingly at the candles flickering in the windows of the rich people's houses they'd walk past. "You were sweet to remember how much I loved the candles."

He put one of those long fingers under her chin to tilt her face up, his dark blue gaze locked on her. "I remember everything about you, Frankie."

"So the wreaths...."

"Just like the one on the door of the posh house in Ballsbridge you loved. The one that you said you were going to buy when you made your fortune."

She swallowed, searching his face for a clue as to why he was doing this. All she saw was the drama of his slashing brows, the strength of his square chin, and the lines etched at the corners of his eyes and mouth. Lines that hadn't been there when they parted twenty-three years before. Lines that only made him more beautiful because they showed he was a man, not a boy.

"Why, Liam?"

"Can't you guess?"

She gave her head a tiny shake so he wouldn't need to release his hold on her. She loved the feel of his finger on the fragile skin that stretched over her jaw.

"I told you when we said good-bye that I would find you—"

"You were a kid then."

"I was no more a kid than you were. We grew up too fast because we had no choice." His eyebrows pulled downward, putting a furrow between them. "I said I would find you, wherever you were."

She held her breath because she remembered what he had said after that.

"I told you I'd find you," he continued, "and convince you to love me."

CHAPTER THREE

His words sent a thrill of longing and denial shivering through Frankie. "You were eighteen. It was a long time ago." She took a step backward.

He matched her step, moving forward to stay near her. He ran his hands up her arms to grip her shoulders. "You can't use my age as an excuse now."

She closed her eyes, savoring the power of his hold on her, letting the heat of his hands sink deep into her body, wishing she didn't feel a hundred years older than the man touching her. "Yes, I can," she whispered. "You deserve a family."

The silence made her open her eyes again. His eyes were lit with tenderness. "You are my family. You always have been."

She started to shake her head.

"Give me a chance, *a stór*. You owe me that."

"I don't owe anyone anything," she said. "All that I have, all that I am, I made myself."

"Don't you want someone to be sharing it with?" His voice was all Irish, a music soft as velvet.

The yearning his words stirred up nearly choked her. She forced her voice past the tightness in her throat, making it sound strong and certain. "I prefer my solitude. I don't compromise well."

Instead of being put off, he laughed. "Now that would be an understatement, if ever there was one." He leaned closer, his voice dropping to a husky murmur. "I'm going to change your mind about solitude, Frankie. I swear it." He released her. "You still have to light the candle."

This time she held the match steady, transferring the flame to the wick so it flared into light. For a moment, she just watched the flame, letting the sweetness of Liam's gesture wash over her like a warm sea.

"Our dinner's waiting for us." He pivoted.

Following his motion, she saw the table set in the middle of the room, draped in green linen and lit by more of the pillar candles, their bases wreathed in garlands of holly and ivy. A plate covered with a silver dome sat at each of the two place settings. Champagne flutes sparkled in the candlelight, and a silver wine cooler stood on its own pedestal.

Liam held the chair for her. The tiny hairs on the back of her neck stirred with pleasure at his nearness. He lifted the cover from her plate and walked to his own seat.

By the time he sat down across from her, Frankie had her armor firmly strapped on again. She touched the jewelry she wore, her favorite gems: black opal and diamond earrings and a triple strand of perfectly matched Mikimoto pearls. She had taken on men just as intimidating as Liam with these talismans and come out the victor.

A waiter in a white jacket materialized at the side of the table. When he plucked out the bottle to fill the paper-thin flutes, she saw that the champagne was Dom Pérignon. Memory flooded her again. When she'd begun to experiment with developing her own chocolates at Balfour Chocolatiers, she'd dreamed of flavoring them with champagne, but couldn't afford the key ingredient. She'd told Liam that she'd know she had made it to the top of her profession when she could use not just any champagne, but Dom Pérignon.

"Your Dom Bombs are my go-to gift," Liam said, proving that his choice of beverage was no accident. "Although my personal favorite is your Black-and-Tan bar." He swirled the champagne in the glass. "The taste of your chocolate makes me feel young."

The urge to plunge a wooden spoon into a vat of rich, thick, melted chocolate made her fingers curl with longing. "I don't make chocolate anymore. Not since I sold Taste of Ireland to Giacometti International."

He set down his glass and pulled his wallet out of his jacket pocket, the movement sending glints of candlelight waltzing along the waves of his thick hair, turning it copper. He extracted a folded newspaper clipping from a compartment in the dark leather billfold and handed it to her.

It was the *Wall Street Journal* article, worn along the creases, announcing the sale of her chocolate business to the Italian firm. She had the same article framed in her penthouse office. It was the day when the world found out that she was a billionaire.

"I tried to send you roses," he said, "but no one would give me your address. I finally sent them to the corporate headquarters of Taste of Ireland, but they said you were already gone."

Something in her chest warmed at the knowledge that he'd tried to celebrate with her.

"Of course, you've always been good at a quick exit." His tone was dry.

"I didn't leave you." He had been the one to go. To the premier league soccer academy that launched him into the stratosphere of his sport. "It was lonely after you were gone."

"Is that why you flew off to America without a word?"

"I had an opportunity and I took it." She looked down at the plate in front of her. "I was afraid you'd leave the academy just to say good-bye. I didn't want you to screw up *your* opportunity."

She risked a glance at him. He sat back in his chair, his broad shoulders framed by the blue leather upholstery. It was hard to read his expression in the wavering candlelight. One moment he looked angry, the next he seemed sad.

"You were always more worried about my career than I was." He gave her a crooked smile. "And I thank you for that."

"You had a great talent, and the passion to go with it. I didn't want you to squander it in Finglas."

"Did you ever think you'd fail?"

She took a sip of champagne, enjoying the fizz that tickled her tongue. "Fail to do what? Get out? No. I knew that I would haul myself out of that pit, but that was setting the bar low." She shrugged. "Anything else was a bonus."

"Bollocks. You always had your sights on world domination."

"All I wanted was so much money that I would never, ever have to think about it again."

"So you don't think about your money?"

"You know the answer to that. Money brings its own burdens." Even though she'd given half her fortune away by putting it into a charitable foundation, it still required substantial attention. "But you have an extra layer of pressure. You have to win."

"Always." His tone held undercurrents that seemed to extend the meaning beyond soccer. But his next words were light. "Neither one of us likes to lose. It's worse than dying because you have to live with it."

She laughed at the sports cliché and then sobered. "Has it gotten any easier, Liam?"

"On the soccer pitch, no." He frowned into his champagne. "But there are certain situations that require patience and tolerance, so I'm learning to be less…intense."

"What situations would those be?"

He nodded toward her plate. "Eat your caviar."

If it were twenty-three years ago, he would have blurted out his secret to her. Liam had always been open with her, even while she had hidden the darker parts of her life from him. So it was strange to have him withhold anything, but he was a grown man now, in more ways than just the physical.

She picked up the tiny mother-of-pearl spoon and scooped up the black beads from their glass dish, dropping them onto the perfectly round, bite-size blini. Popping the blini between her lips, she let the aroma fill her mouth and then pressed her tongue upward to pop the firm eggs against her palate. They released their rich, buttery flavor of salt. Definitely Ossetra, one of the best.

"You still eat the same way," Liam said. "With your eyes closed to concentrate on the taste."

"Only when the food is worth the effort." After the deprivations of her childhood, she'd had to train herself not to gulp down food. So now she chewed slowly and with attention.

He looked pleased. "I told the chef to make sure the flavors were unique and interesting. He seemed confident about everything except the dessert. I insisted on chocolate."

"You told him who I am."

"It will inspire him to up his game." He took a bite of caviar, chewed, and swallowed. "Tell me about the Bellwether Club."

She started to give him her well-rehearsed tale about the fancy clubs rejecting her because she was a woman, Irish, and new money. How she'd resolved to found her own ultra-exclusive place and make it the clubbiest damned club in New York City, open only to those who had made their ten-figure fortunes entirely from scratch. But Liam wouldn't let her laugh about it. He drew out the pain of those rejections, took only honesty from her. And she felt lighter once she'd made the confession to him.

"What about you?" she asked, as they ate a salad of papaya, beans, and crushed peanuts with a tangy coriander dressing. "What did you thumb your nose at?"

He shook his head, making a curve of thick auburn hair fall onto his forehead. She wanted to brush it back, as she had in the old days, when she allowed herself only small touches so she wouldn't be tempted to more. "It wasn't sports that hurt me. For all that I hate to lose, I know that someone has to in every game." He trapped her in the blaze of his deep blue eyes. "I kept hoping I'd hear from you. But you never answered my calls or my emails."

"I had an international business to run in the U.S. You had an elite sports career in Europe." It took all her willpower to keep her voice firm, just as it had taken all her willpower not to answer his calls. But she'd been afraid to talk with him, fearful that her self-discipline would collapse under the weight of her feelings for him. "What would have been the point?"

"Oh, I don't know. Friendship?" His tone was pure sarcasm.

"You wanted more, and I didn't have it to give."

He leaned forward. "I'd have settled for a word every now and then. Just to know you remembered your oldest mate."

"I have a box in my safe of every news story ever written about you, every photo ever taken, every magazine cover you were on. I know all the teams you played for, the championships you won...or lost, the contracts you signed." The wags he'd dated, but she wouldn't admit that to him.

Surprise and gratification danced across his face.

"I kept watching for an engagement announcement, too. You're wealthy, famous, and good-looking. I was sure you'd be married by now."

He seemed to flinch before he forced a smile that was meant to be wicked. "I'm glad you noticed the good-looking part."

"I'm not dead, just disciplined."

"Why the discipline? Don't throw the age difference at me again. We're both old enough so it doesn't matter."

"It matters because you can and should have children. You always wanted them."

He turned to stare at the windows that reflected the flickering candle flames. "And you didn't because you felt that all those babies destroyed your ma and took away any hope she had of a better life."

He didn't know how much deeper it went. She'd never told him about how she lay awake listening to her little sisters and brothers crying with hunger at night. She'd taken to giving them as much of her own food as she could without starving herself. Even being careful, she'd blacked out from hunger a few times in school. The nurse had been kind enough to blame it on low blood sugar, giving Frankie a few graham crackers to wolf down.

She'd dropped out of school to work at Balfour Chocolatiers because she couldn't bear to see the children's huge hungry eyes staring at her, pleading, as she ladled out the tiny portions of the dinner she'd scraped together. She didn't tell her da about the job so she could keep the money to buy food for all of them. And every now and then she got to bring home rejected chocolates, a treat that made her siblings look upon her as nothing short of an angel.

But she still heard their thin, desperate voices, crying, in her nightmares, and it brought back the old, throat-clutching feeling that her siblings were starving, and she couldn't save them.

She was grateful when Liam's voice broke into those memories. "But you made more than enough money to hire all the help you needed," he said.

"Do you know how many hours a day I spent at home while I was running Taste of Ireland? Maybe six and most of that was to sleep. In fact, I often slept in my office." She toyed with a slice of papaya.

"If I'd had children, they'd never have seen me. I wouldn't do that to a kid."

"You'd have a husband."

"And he wouldn't have seen me either." All the familiar frustration vibrated through her. "You can't have it all. You have to make choices in life, especially if you're a woman."

He had the grace to look sympathetic. "I don't deny it. But if anyone could have managed both work and family, it's you."

"Don't be a bloody gobdaw," Frankie said, weariness blunting any edge in her insult. "I had to work twice as hard as any man, just because I don't have a Y chromosome."

He held up his hand in surrender. "It's a man's world. God knows I work in a sea of testosterone."

"I'd rather not fight with an old friend. Let's talk about your team," Frankie said, tamping down her anger. "You've got a solid midfielder in Graham Bradley."

Liam hesitated a moment, as though he was going to argue with her change of topic. But then he gave a half-shrug. "Graham certainly thinks so. I'm more interested in Kyle Hyndman. He's going to be a standout with the right coaching."

"So it's your coaching that will be making him great, is it?"

Liam raised his eyebrows. "Everyone knows it's the coach who turns a team into champions."

She snorted. "You told me it was the center midfielder who won championships."

"And it was…when I was the center midfielder."

Frankie relaxed. As long as she didn't touch him, she could settle into their old, easy dynamic, and let the physical pull of him recede to just a simmer in her veins. It felt good to spar with him, to hear the lilt of their home in his voice, and even to let the Irish filter into her own. She hadn't called anyone a gobdaw in years.

After she'd complimented the chef on the clever chocolate soccer balls filled with spice-infused chocolate mousse, Liam brought out her coat. "Let's step into the outside box and get some fresh air."

He held open the glass door leading to the rows of cushioned outdoor seats that looked out on the silent, snow-covered baseball field. She could see the outline of the diamond under the coating of white. She drew in a lungful of crisp, winter air and blew it out in a cloud of vapor.

Liam stood with his hands shoved deep into his overcoat pockets, his gaze on the huge expanse of the empty arena. "I'm going to make the New York Challenge so exciting to watch that we'll fill every one of those 50,000 seats by the end of the season."

"You're playing the wrong kind of football to do that in the U.S.," Frankie said. "If you sell 30,000 tickets you'll be doing well."

He shook his head. "New York loves winners, and I promise you we're going to make the playoffs."

This was a Liam she hadn't seen before. A man forged and tested in the fiery competition of the top tier of professional sports. His confidence was born of being a champion many times over.

Suddenly, she felt a shift in their relationship. He was her equal now. And that was a dangerous thing.

Liam held the limousine door for Frankie while he inwardly cursed himself. He'd screwed up somehow. He'd felt Frankie soften through dinner, but then he'd taken her outside to impress her with his new kingdom, and all the walls had come back up again.

He should have realized that fancy locations wouldn't win her over. After all, she was so rich that she had access to almost any venue she wanted. The chocolate dessert had been a point for him, though. And the candle. He hadn't seen Frankie cry more than twice in the years he'd known her.

As he slid onto the back seat beside her, he sifted through other options. Frankie was the one who'd told him that there were many paths to the goal, and he needed to have his eye on the whole field to see them all. He'd put her advice to work in becoming the best center midfielder in the premier league. But he'd known even then that she was talking about more than just soccer.

The limo had gone about three blocks before he formulated a new approach.

"You've gone quiet. Planning your strategy for filling all those seats?" Frankie asked with a smile.

"No," he said. She had moved into the corner of the limo, half-turning so she could look directly at him. He hated every inch of the space between them. "I'm planning our day out tomorrow."

She raised her finely arched eyebrows at him. "I have a club to run."

"It's Sunday, the day of rest."

"Ha! When you're in the hospitality business, there is no rest."

Donal had told him that Sundays were quiet at the Bellwether Club. Most of the high achievers who frequented it did so during the business week. "Surely, you trust your staff to handle things for a few hours." His tone was a deliberate challenge.

"Why tomorrow?" she asked with her usual brutal directness.

Because it was her voice he had heard encouraging him when the coach reamed him out and he wanted to quit the academy. It was her face he saw when his aching body kept him awake after a long, miserable practice or a dirty, hard-fought game. And nowadays, it was her toughness he channeled when coaching a prima donna of a player who forgot there was no "I" in "team". Sometimes he would close his eyes and imagine he could even feel the way her body had fit against him their last day together. The time she'd kissed him with a desperate longing that had matched his.

"Because I'm new here, and I want some company to go exploring with," he said. "Who better than my oldest mate?"

"I'm sure you could round up plenty of company," she said, her tone dry. Then her face softened and she rested her hand on his forearm. "It's so good to see you again, Liam."

"I'm going to be staying here in the city." He didn't like that she looked at him as though he were a ghost or a memory, not a living, breathing man. "So I expect to see you often."

She just shook her head and started to pull her hand away. He covered it, holding it in place, savoring the feel of her delicate bones against his palm. "It's the Christmas season, Frankie. I want to spend it with someone who's like family to me."

Her fingertips pressed into his arm. "Would I be your sister or a favorite aunt?"

"More like a very distant cousin, the kissing kind. There's mistletoe aplenty this time of year."

She leaned toward him and lifted her free hand to brush a hank of his hair back, the feel of her fingers against the skin of his temple sending a rope of heat straight down to his groin.

"I can't decide if seeing you makes me feel old or young," she said.

He gave her his best roguish grin. "You'll find out tomorrow, I promise you."

CHAPTER FOUR

Pure lust flashed through Frankie when she saw Liam standing in her office's anteroom the next morning, his long legs wrapped in worn jeans that showed every contour of his powerful thigh muscles, and a cream Aran sweater that hugged the curves of his wide shoulders. His gaze skimmed over her, leaving a trail of heat. "You can't wear that to go sledding," he said.

"Sledding!" Frankie had expected a trip to see the tree at Rockefeller Center at worst, so she'd worn tailored wool trousers and a cashmere sweater. "I'm not twelve years old."

He grinned at her, a flash of straight, white teeth. "When I saw the fresh snow this morning, it brought out the kid in me. So the kid in you is coming along too."

She considered refusing. But his smile pulled at something buried deep within her. "If I break a bone, you have to nurse me back to health."

The blue of his eyes turned incandescent. "Gladly," he said, his voice taking on a husky edge. "I imagine you'll need lots of sponge baths."

A vision of his hand wrapped around a wet, soapy sponge as he ran it over her bare breasts sent a ribbon of arousal twisting into her belly. "I'll hire a nurse."

Liam slanted a glinting smile at her. "And I was planning such a nice sled crash for us. Now, off you go to dress properly."

It would be rude to leave him alone downstairs while she went up to her apartment to change, but she wasn't sure she was ready to let him into her private sanctuary. However, he was Liam. "Come up with me in case you have further opinions on my attire."

He nodded and followed her to the private elevator. His big athlete's body took up more than half the space, so their shoulders and arms bumped together.

"Good thing I'm not claustrophobic," he said, snaking his arm around her shoulders before he winked down at her. "We take up less space closer together."

Oh dear God, she was pressed against him from knee to shoulder, his body a solid wall of heat and muscle, while the band of his arm fell strong and weighty across her shoulders. Through the thin cashmere of her sweater, his fingers seemed to burn their outline onto the skin of her upper arm.

She nearly gasped in relief when the doors opened onto her foyer. She stepped forward, but Liam kept his arm around her, matching her stride with his before he brought them both to a halt just inside the living room.

As he looked around her home, he exploded into laughter so uproarious she felt the vibration of it through her body.

She'd built her apartment on top of the ornate old brownstone that housed the Bellwether Club, but her place was all clean, modern lines, walls of glass, and soaring ceilings with skylights, so light poured in no matter what time of day it was.

"And here I was thinking that you had bought into all that English nob's decorating downstairs, but no, you're just making fun of it." Liam squinted against the sunlight reflecting off the snow drifting on her rooftop terrace. "You always hated the grayness of Dublin."

"Control, shades on half," Frankie barked. The glass windows rippled into a tinted gray, cutting the glare of the winter sun.

Liam whistled and released her, strolling over to the quilted maple shelves that lined one wall. He stopped in front of a grouping of photographs, his hands tucked into the back pockets of his jeans. For a long moment, he surveyed the pictures. Then he pulled his hands free and picked up one framed photo.

When he lifted his head to meet her gaze, he had a strange, arrested look on his face that made her stomach twist. This was why she shouldn't have brought him up here.

"I have the other half of this," he said. "I didn't think...didn't expect.... You kept them." He traced a finger over the two small photos of them, their faces pressed cheek to cheek, taken in a photo booth in Dublin the day he'd left for the soccer training academy in England.

"I've got a streak of the Irish sentimentality. I just keep it under control," she said. In fact, she had an enlarged version of the photos in her bedroom, but he didn't need to know that.

He set the frame down. "Bundle up. It's going to be cold and windy beside the Hudson."

"The Hudson? I thought people went sledding in Central Park."

"Serious sliders go to Riverside Park at 91st Street."

"I think I need a bunny slope."

"We're headed for Suicide Hill."

His challenging smile made it hard to decide if he was joking or not, so she ignored him and headed into her bedroom. She hauled a pair of jeans out of a far corner of her closet and added a cotton thermal turtleneck layered under a heavy cashmere sweater. Her winter boots all had high heels, so she settled on a pair of pull-on paddock boots, left over from the days she'd ridden horseback in Central Park. She chortled with satisfaction over the fancy fur-trimmed ski jacket she'd bought before she realized she had no interest in skiing. She'd get some use out of it at last.

When she walked out of the bedroom, Liam was standing in front of the sliding glass door that led onto the terrace. He pivoted on his heel. "You've got a nice setup here." He grinned. "Want to rent it to me?"

"You don't have a place yet?"

"I'm staying at the Brownstone Inn on 82nd while I look for something." He shrugged. "It's got working fireplaces and a lobby with a Christmas tree. Speaking of which, where is your tree? You've got garlands and wreaths strung up all over the place in the club, but not a sprig of holiday cheer up here."

"I don't like clutter." She hadn't put up a Christmas tree in years. It seemed like too much work when the only person who saw it was herself.

"Now I know what else we'll be doing today." He let his eyes roam over her again, but this time she knew it was just to inspect her sledding ensemble, so she quelled any reaction.

"You'll do," he said, sweeping them into the elevator and through the club to the limousine waiting outside the front door.

"A limo to go sledding? That seems wrong."

"It gets crowded at Suicide Hill so we don't want to worry about parking."

She slid into the car to discover a long Flexible Flyer sled resting upside down across the leather seat behind the driver. The incongruity of it made her laugh.

"You're enjoying yourself already." Liam sounded pleased.

"There's only one sled. Are we taking turns?"

He scooted close to her on the seat. "We're in this together. We'll go faster that way."

The limo driver found a spot by a fire hydrant so they could unload the sled. Liam carried it across the sidewalk to the top of the hill, where a bundled-up crowd of mostly teenagers stood waiting for an opening to head down the slope. As she and Liam joined them, Frankie looked downward to discover a steep incline dotted with trees and speeding sliders whose shrieks and laughter rang through the ice-clear air. At the bottom a line of hay bales cushioned the metal fence that guarded them from a plunge into the frigid gray waters of the Hudson River. While she watched, a sled slammed into a bare tree, spilling its rider off into the snow and dumping the snow from the tree's branches on top of him.

"This looks dangerous," she said, releasing her breath only when the rider stood up and brushed at the splotches of white on his clothes.

"It looks like a helluva good run." His face was lit with excitement and he rubbed his gloved hands together in anticipation. "I think it's best if I lie down on my stomach and you lie on top of me. That will keep our center of gravity lower, so the steering is better."

"I'd say that you'll give me a soft cushion to land on, but there's not much soft about your body." And she'd be lying full-length against it. Luckily, there would be many layers of fabric between them.

His eyes blazed, but he turned back to the slope. "Ah, I think we have an opening." He positioned the sled on the flat space at the top of the park. "I'll get on the sled. You give us a push and then jump on top of me."

With that he dropped to his knees and stretched out on his belly on the Flexible Flyer, his shoulders jutting out over the sides and his legs extending far beyond its end. She almost sent him down without her, but the truth was that she wanted to feel the long, solid length of him against her. "Ready?" she asked, stooping to set her hands on his waist.

"Do it!"

She dug her toes into the snow, giving Liam a sharp shove forward. Then she hurled herself on top of his back as the sled tilted its nose downward and began to move.

The runners hissed over the well-packed snow and the wind drew tears from the corners of her eyes as the sled picked up speed. But her awareness was focused on the way his hair tickled her cheeks as it blew back, the way his shoulders bunched under her hands when he yanked the sled's steering bar right to avoid a fallen sledder, and how delicious it was to have her breasts crushed against the warm, solid wall of his back.

And then he was rolling, taking her off the sled with him just before it slammed into the protective hay bales. Now he was on top of her, braced on his forearms and laughing, while their legs tangled in the churned up snow. "A good first run, but we can do better," he said, leaping up and hauling her to her feet before they got taken out by less controlled sliders.

He grabbed the sled's rope and then her hand, pulling both of them over to the side for the trudge back up the slope. By the time they reached the top, she was gasping for breath.

"I see I'm going to have to get you to the gym more often," Liam said, as she bent over, her hands on her knees.

"It's just that you have longer legs than I do."

When she straightened, there was no laughter on his face. "Frankie, you have to take care of yourself."

"Do you call this mad hurtle down a slope filled with crazed teenagers taking care of yourself?"

He looked at the people launching themselves down the hill with wild enthusiasm. "Yeah, I do. Because this is the kind of pure fun I couldn't allow myself when I was on a team. I couldn't ice skate or ski or play basketball or rugby, for fear of getting injured. Golf was about as rough-and-tumble as it got, and even then I took care with my back. I missed playing something, anything, just for the pleasure of it." His gaze returned to her. "What kind of fun did you get up to when you were building your empire?"

Frankie snorted. "My idea of a good time was dreaming up new kinds of chocolate bars, experimenting with flavors, fighting my way into new markets. Watching my bank account go up and up and up until I knew I would never have to return to Finglas."

"But you did return to Finglas. You built that cooking school that's free to kids like us."

"I never set foot in it. I sent people I trusted to make it happen. When I got on the plane to Philadelphia, I made myself a promise that I would leave that life behind me. Even for a good cause, I wasn't going back again."

He dropped the sled's rope and cupped her shoulders in his big hands. "I know it was hard for you. Your da was a right bastard, and your ma had all those kids to take care of. But we had some good times there in Finglas, you and I."

"Once you got the scholarship for the training academy, you were gone, and I hoped to God you wouldn't be coming back." She hadn't realized how hard it would be without Liam there. Not only because he always had her back, but because he had never once laughed at her dreams. "I missed the hell out of you."

He pulled her into his arms, cradling her head against his chest. "Ah, God, I would lie on my hard cot in the academy digs at night, aching to see you, to hear your voice. It was like my heart had been ripped out and left behind."

She did it again. Allowed herself to lean into his strength before she lifted her head out of his supporting hand and looked him in the eye with a wry smile. "A pathetic pair we were, then."

Instead of laughing, his mouth went thin with anger. "Don't dismiss what we felt for each other. It was a powerful thing for the good, not a weakness in us."

"It hurt so badly that I wasn't sure I would live through it." She'd never told another soul how close she'd been to giving up in the months after Liam had gone off to seek his bright future. She'd walked the dirty, cracked sidewalks beside the walls covered in obscene graffiti and wondered if she would ever claw her way out.

"I never wanted to cause you pain, *a stór*. Never."

That little hitch vibrated in her chest, scaring her, but she refused to flinch. "You didn't hurt me. Our grim, stingy life did. Because I cared about you I had to let you go. We didn't deserve to be that poor. No one does."

His embrace tightened and she let him shelter her, from the bitter river wind, from the chattering teenagers, from the feelings threatening to drown her. It had been a long time since she'd felt protected by another human being.

"Liam Keller? Aren't you Liam Keller, the new coach for the New York Challenge?" An excited but refined male voice shattered the moment of stillness.

Liam's hold loosened but he didn't release her. Instead he turned and tucked her against his side as he faced a dark-haired man wearing a ski jacket and red scarf, and holding a microphone. Behind the reporter a scruffy cameraman carried a video cam marked "WNYN News".

The reporter held out his hand, "I'm Mark Singh with WNYN. I'm doing a local color piece on New Yorkers enjoying the snowfall, and I'd love to include you in it. Would you give me a couple of minutes of your time?"

Liam shook his hand and gave Frankie a rueful smile. "Sure thing, Mark."

"Great! So tell us what brings you here?"

She could feel Liam gather himself before he flashed his famous smile and said, "I'm enjoying one of the simple pleasures of my new home city." A mild obscenity sounded from the hill behind them, making Liam chuckle. "And learning some American colloquialisms."

"You know this is called 'Suicide Hill'? Have you been down it yet?" Mark asked.

"That we have, and a fine, fast ride it was." Frankie nearly laughed as Liam struck the perfect balance between his Irish accent and being understood by an American audience. "We dodged all the trees and thanked God for the hay bales at the bottom."

"And you, ma'am, what did you think of the hill?" Mark thrust the mic at Frankie.

Liam's grip on her waist tightened, but Frankie had faced plenty of television cameras in her day. "I was glad I had an elite level athlete with great reflexes at the helm. There are no traffic rules on that slope."

"Sounds like you're from Ireland too," Mark said.

"Liam and I are friends from way back," she said with a nod.

Mark turned to the camera. "And that was Liam Keller, newly hired coach of the New York Challenge. Now we know how he spends his time when he's not on the soccer pitch."

The red recording light on the camera winked out, and Mark said, "I'm a soccer fan myself. Good luck with your new team."

Liam dug into his jeans pocket for his wallet, pulling a business card out of it. "Drop me an email, and I'll make sure you get good seats."

"That's a deal," Mark said, tucking the card in his coat's inner pocket. "Don't break anything. New Yorkers go a little crazy in the snow."

The reporter wandered off, trailing his cameraman. Liam stood watching, his smile still in place, until Mark was out of sight.

"Jaysus, you can't escape the media anywhere," he muttered.

"That's why the Bellwether Club exists."

"But you can't go sledding there." He shrugged off his irritation and nudged the sled with his foot. "Ready for another run?"

"It's my turn to steer."

"I thought you were happy to have an elite athlete driving for you."

"The first time down."

"All right then." He grinned. "But I don't think you want me to be lying on top of you, so we'll do it sitting, with you in the front in full control."

He was wrong about her not wanting him on top of her, but it was a thought she shouldn't be having.

He pulled the sled to the lip of the slope and held it while Frankie seated herself with her feet braced against the steering bar. He sat behind her, bringing his long legs up on either side of her and bending them so his knees nearly reached her shoulders. It was like having a railing made of denim-covered muscle.

"I'm going to give us a shove so brace yourself," he said, his voice coming from beside her right ear so the warmth of his breath feathered over her skin.

The sled slid back a few inches before jerking forward with a powerful lurch and hurtling down the slope. Liam leaned into her, so his chest was solid against her back and his arms were wrapped around her waist. But she had no time to enjoy the feel of him enveloping her, as the wind brought tears to her eyes and scoured her cheeks with cold.

The tree trunks and fellow sledders came up fast so she had to focus on weaving among them, the tree trunks more easily than the sledders because they didn't suddenly veer in unexpected directions. But the speed! The speed was delicious, and the risk made her blood fizz with exhilaration.

The hay bales came at them, and Liam threw himself sideways, taking her with him. For a moment, she lay on top of him, laughing. "Again!" she cried.

"As often as you want."

While they slogged up the hill with the sled, Frankie felt something in her open up, like a door allowing a sliver of light into a dark room. She reached for Liam's gloved hand. "Thank you for bringing me."

His fingers curled around hers as though he held a precious artifact. "You're the reason I came."

Half a dozen downward plunges later, Liam was lying under her and steering along the edge of the slope when a pair of teenaged boys, who were headed back up the hill, stepped out in front of them. Liam cursed a blue streak as he tried to wrench the sled away from the kids. Suddenly, the boys separated and lifted their sled up over their heads, making an arch for Liam and Frankie to pass under. As their sled whooshed through the opening, Liam gave them a piece of his mind in Gaelic. The boys cheered and Frankie laughed.

When they toppled off the sled at the bottom of the slope, Liam was still muttering about stupid, feckless teenagers.

"Come on, those kids gave us the perfect finish," Frankie said. "A triumphal arch." She looked up the hill but couldn't find the daring pair in the crowd.

"Are you saying you're done?"

"It seems the right note to end on. That and the fact that my fingers are going numb."

"Let's get you into the heat of the limo." As they walked up the hill, he called the driver, so the car was waiting when they arrived at the crest.

Liam wrestled the sled back into the car, making Frankie chuckle as she bent to get in too. "I can't get used to a sled in a limo," she said.

"Wait until you see it with your Christmas tree tied on the top." He took one of her hands and peeled the glove off. "Yup, your fingers are red with cold. Give me your other hand too." He sandwiched her hands between his big palms, sharing the warmth of his skin with her. It felt strangely safe to have her hands trapped in his.

"I don't have any decorations for a tree."

"That's easy to fix."

She pulled her hands out from his. "When I need Christmas cheer I just go downstairs."

"Remember what happened to Scrooge."

"I give everyone who works for me a Christmas turkey."

He laughed, his cold-reddened cheeks creasing. "What's the ceiling height on your elevator? About seven feet?"

"I don't need a tree that big."

"You could put a twenty-foot tree in that apartment of yours."

"And it would take a small army with ladders to hang ornaments on it."

He slung his arm around her shoulders and gave her a little shake. "Did you have fun sledding?"

"You're now going to use specious logic on me. Since I enjoyed the sledding, I will enjoy the Christmas tree."

"And there you have it." He pulled her against his side. "Give it up, Frankie. You know I'm as fiercely stubborn as you are."

She laughed because she couldn't deny it. Of course, their biggest arguments had always been about her walking home late after work at the chocolatier. Liam had insisted that she needed an escort, and she'd told him she was a grown woman and could take care of herself.

And she could, until the night her boss had agreed to let her develop her own line of chocolates. She'd floated through the gray, dimly lit streets, her mind on flavors and shapes and textures. Pure joy had flowed through her, the kind that made you forget everything but the moment. The kind that made anything seem possible. The kind she was feeling right now, with Liam's strong arm around her.

But that was the night she'd nearly been raped. If Liam hadn't come to her rescue, God knows if she'd even still be alive.

In the years since, she'd allowed herself to feel triumph or satisfaction or gratification, but never again that kind of blind happiness. It made you stupid and vulnerable, and she couldn't afford either.

CHAPTER FIVE

The snow-dusted Christmas trees leaned against temporary fencing set up on a parking lot. Couples in bright hats and puffy jackets, some with children in tow, strolled through the fragrant outdoor aisles in search of the perfect pine.

A ho-ho-ho-ing Santa Claus greeted Frankie and Liam on the sidewalk in front of the cashier's shed. "And what do you want for Christmas, little lady?" he asked.

That stymied Frankie. She could buy whatever she wanted, so there wasn't anything left to put on her list. "World peace," she said.

"That's a tall order," Santa said. "But I'll do my best."

As Santa went on to the next customer, Liam said, "Such an altruist you are."

"It's better for the chocolate business if people aren't shooting at each other."

"Is there nothing you want?"

She waved her hand in dismissal. "I've got all the jets and diamonds I can use."

"I keep forgetting that you could buy a small country, if you chose. For now, we'll settle for a tree."

She noticed that he had stiffened and the teasing light had vanished from his face. He had a problem with her money? That seemed ironic, since their youthful dreams had always been about being rich.

But Liam was already walking down the rows of trees propped against the wooden fence. Frankie watched as he occasionally grabbed a fir and stood it upright for inspection before letting it drop back again.

"What's wrong with that one?" she asked after the seventh tree had been rejected.

"Not fat enough. Maybe they have one that hasn't been opened up yet." He waved at one of the men working at the lot. "Hey, do you have a seven-footer that's got some girth?"

The fellow strolled up. "I might have one still netted…hey, aren't you Liam Keller? Man, you are the best!" He raised his voice. "Yo, Pete, it's Liam Keller."

"What? You're puttin' me—" A short, chubby man in an orange ski jacket came to a halt in front of them with his mouth hanging open. "Liam effing Keller."

"Nice to meet you, Pete," Liam said with a half-smile. "I take it you're a soccer fan."

"I'm a big fan of *yours*," Pete said, finding his voice and shaking Liam's hand. "When you scored that goal in the final against Germany…." He shook his head in wonder. "Okay, Rich, get this man the best tree on the lot. You want seven feet? You got eight."

Frankie trailed the trio to a pile of newly delivered trees behind the cashier's shed, listening to them relive various moments of glory in Liam's career. She was surprised at his celebrity here in New York. If he'd been a baseball player, she would have expected the recognition, but soccer wasn't so popular in the States.

Rich, Pete, and Liam cut open several trees before they agreed that *this* was what they were looking for. "What do you think, Frankie?" Liam asked, walking around the tree as Pete held it.

"I've never seen a better one."

"I like you," Rich said, giving her a thumbs-up. "Let's get it on your car." When he saw the limo, he whistled. "Mr. Keller knows how to do things in style."

Once the tree was secured, Frankie was pressed into service to take pictures with Rich's and Pete's phones of the two of them with Liam and the limo. Then Liam asked Pete to take a picture of him and Frankie together with Liam's phone. Frankie caught herself smoothing her hair like a teenager and stopped as Liam put his arm around her shoulders. "Smile, my pretty bird," he said.

That made her laugh just as Pete took the shot. "I haven't been called a bird in donkey's years."

"About time someone did it then," Liam said, folding himself into the limousine beside her.

"Ha!" But she felt a little glow of pleasure that he thought of her as a girl. Which was ridiculous for a woman of her years. "Your fame has preceded you to New York, I see. Before long you'll be on the cover of *People Magazine*."

"I hear I have a good shot at Sexiest Man Alive this year," he said, but his attention was on his phone where he was swiping away.

"I'd smack you for your conceit but it's probably true."

He raised his head, his blue eyes hot and amused. "That's twice now."

"Twice?"

"That you've commented on my incredible good looks. It's a good sign."

"It's just a fact."

He lifted an eyebrow and went back to his phone, scrolling and tapping until he made a final grand flourish. "There. Now we're headed for the proper store to buy decorations for your tree. And we can go back to talking about my handsomeness."

She punched him in the arm, surprising herself but making him chuckle. "Seriously, Liam, you're bloody famous."

"Which can be bloody inconvenient." He sighed. "I'm not complaining, mind you. I just didn't expect it so soon here. The truth is that I need all the fans and media coverage I can get when it comes to putting soccer on the map in the States."

"I'm going to introduce you to a friend of mine. He plays the wrong kind of football, but he's got powerful connections in the professional sports world."

Liam frowned. "And who might this footballer be?"

"Luke Archer. He's the quarterback for—"

"I know who Luke Archer is. The question is: How do *you* know him?"

"He's a member of the Bellwether Club, of course." Frankie was amused by his fit of jealousy. She'd come to know Luke well because he was one of the three crazy gamblers from her club who'd made a bet on true love. She was rooting for all of them to win their wager of hearts, but she couldn't share their secret, even with Liam.

"You keep impressive company." Liam didn't look happy about that.

"I'm almost invisible to my members. As long as things are going smoothly, they don't even know I'm there."

"That's been your choice all along."

"It's easier that way. You don't build a billion-dollar company from the ground up without making a few enemies."

His eyes turned glacial, but he said nothing. Not like the old days, when he would have demanded she give him their names, so he could warn them off. "I have my own connections," he said.

Pride. He'd always had it in spades. Sometimes that was all that had kept him from giving up, so she couldn't fault him for it. "I imagine you do. All over the world, in fact."

"Thanks for the offer of an introduction, though." The ice melted and the gleam of humor reappeared. "You wouldn't by any chance know J.K. Rowling personally, would you?"

"Can't help you with that one. You're a Harry Potter fan?"

"No, but I know someone who is." He turned to look out the window but not before she caught the look of discomfort that crossed his face. "Here we are."

Liam hustled her across the sidewalk and through the door before she could read the store's sign. As she stepped inside, she had the sense of being inside a kaleidoscope, with brilliant bursts of translucent color surrounding her.

"Welcome to Glass Dreams." A young man in jeans and a black tee shirt stepped out of the swirl of color. "If you have any questions, just ask."

Liam pointed upward. "These would go with your apartment."

Frankie tilted her head back. Globes of blown glass in brilliant colors and patterns hung from multihued silk ribbons. Some had swirls and stripes of colored glass applied to the outside. Some had sculptural shapes inside them. Each one was a work of art in its own right.

"How did you know about this place?" she asked.

That same odd shadow flitted over his face. "I was Christmas shopping in the neighborhood and noticed it. The colors catch your eye from the outside."

"They're brilliant." She ran a quick calculation in her head based on the size of the tree and the density of the branches and spoke to the salesperson. "I'll need about seventy of these. Do you have ornament boxes?"

The young man's eyes lit up before he nodded and disappeared into a back room.

"Point to the ones you want and I'll unhook them," Liam said.

"You have to help choose them too. What do you think of doing the whole tree in different shades of red?"

"No fun. Let's just pick the ones we like the best." He pointed to one that had green and white swirls. "That one reminds me of my first soccer team's colors."

Frankie nodded and Liam took it down.

A black orb with gold speckles swung near her eye level. "Those are the colors of my Black-and-Tan candy bar wrapper."

The young man appeared beside her, a large box with nests of tissue paper resting in his arms. Liam laid the two ornaments in it.

"This one for the Irish rain," Frankie said, pointing to a sphere with silver dripping down its sides.

"Now you're getting into the spirit of it." Liam unhooked a globe spangled with red, white, and blue. "For our new country, the land of opportunity."

The young man fetched fresh boxes as they filled them. When they were finished, the number of silk ribbons dangling with empty ends was noticeable in the small boutique. "No problem," the young man said. "We've got plenty more in the stockroom."

As he began to tally the bill, he looked up at Frankie. "I'm giving you a volume discount."

"I appreciate the Christmas spirit, but charge me full price," Frankie said. "Your glassblowers need it more than I do."

"Especially since this is on me," Liam said, passing his credit card to the sales clerk.

"No!" She'd let him pay for the tree because she wasn't going to argue about it in front of his two new fans, but she would not permit him to fund the extravagance of thousands of dollars in glass decorations. "It's my tree."

"And it's my Christmas gift to you, to make up for all the Christmases I didn't give you a present."

"I didn't give you presents either."

"I've been meaning to speak with you about that," Liam said. "You owe me."

That was so ridiculous that Frankie coughed out a laugh. But she hauled her wallet out of her pocket and pushed a credit card across the counter. "Put the ornaments on my card, or I won't take them."

The sales clerk looked back and forth between them, as he held a credit card in each hand. "Ma'am…sir…I…."

"You're torturing the poor lad," Liam said.

"No more than you are. How about we split the bill? I figure you forced me to get a tree so you should be on the hook for some of the expense."

"You win." He nodded to the clerk. "Half on each card."

"I didn't win, so don't pretend otherwise."

"You noticed that, did you? I should know better than to try to out-negotiate the woman who sold her company for a billion dollars."

The clerk's eyes went wide and he glanced up at Frankie, who shook her head with a pitying smile at Liam. "You know the Irish. Always making up stories. Next he'll tell you he's the superstar soccer player Liam Keller."

"Um, he is." The clerk held up Liam's credit card with his name on it.

"He has the same name and bears a slight resemblance to the man, but that's as far as it goes. He couldn't hit the broad side of a barn with a soccer ball."

The young sales clerk looked like a deer in headlights. "Yes, ma'am. I mean, no, ma'am."

Frankie glanced up at Liam to see his shoulders shaking and the corner of his mouth twitching. She arched an eyebrow at him and signed her credit card slip.

"Um, how do you want me to bag the ornaments?" the young man asked, looking at the pile of their purchases. "There's an uneven number of boxes."

"We'll sort that out ourselves," Liam said. "Bag them however works best."

When they were back in the limo, Liam exploded into laughter. "You're the very devil. 'Couldn't hit the broad side of a barn with a soccer ball.' I had a coach say that to me once after I missed a penalty kick."

"You deserved it for being such a pain in the ass about paying for the decorations."

His laughter stopped as though she'd slammed a door on it. "You know, I could buy you several hundred of those balls without having to live on the street."

"I know, I know. You were being sweet." She reached up to touch his cheek, but he jerked his head back.

"I was not…being…*sweet*. I was attempting to demonstrate that I am a man of the world with excellent taste and significant financial resources."

Maybe she did still think of him as the kid to whom she sometimes gave chocolates that Balfour's had rejected as not perfect enough. Yet she knew he made millions from endorsements and contracts. In fact, he'd probably had more money than she did, when she was in the early years of building Taste of Ireland. "I'm used to paying my own way," she said.

He turned to her with a sharp movement. "That's my point, Frankie. You don't have to when you're with me."

"Give me time. I have to catch up with this new Liam. I knew the old one so well. This one is strange to me." And she'd had to work so hard to be the person she was. Her strength and independence had served her well. It wasn't something she could—or even wanted to—let go of.

"Patience was never one of my virtues." He lifted his hands to thread them into her hair on either side of her face, tilting and holding her head. He waited a breath and then brought his mouth down on hers, his lips warm and firm and challenging. This was not an old friend's kiss. It was not a question. It was an assertion that shivered down her spine and back up again to send ripples of sensation cascading down her shoulders and over the swell of her breasts before it crashed and pooled in her belly. He slanted his lips against hers and painted a line along the seam with his tongue, letting her know he wanted more.

Her body seemed to expand and unfurl, like a desert plant in a sudden rainstorm, soaking up the water it had been deprived of for so long. She felt herself softening, melting into him so she could feel more of his heat and power. A strange sound rose up in her throat, a cross between a sigh and a moan, and she opened her lips to touch his tongue with hers.

He made a sound too, but his was a deep, growling rumble that vibrated into her mouth as they tasted each other. And then his hands were gone from her face, and he was dragging her across his thighs, so she felt the steely muscles in them as she sat on his lap. And she was licking the skin behind his ear while inhaling the scent of warm, clean man with a hint of some exotic citrus shampoo wafting from the waves of his hair. She wanted to laugh and cry at the same time.

He tilted his head sideways as she kissed along his jawline, the angle of it both familiar and strange. "Ahh, Frankie, *a stór.*"

She ran her hands over the patterns and cables of his sweater, hating the bulk of it, wanting to find the contours of his muscles, the satin of his skin. And then his arms went around her and he kissed the same places on her, flicking her neck with his tongue so delight danced through her. She buried her fingers in the thick glory of his hair as he bent to her, the strands stroking her like silk. Every sensation, every touch he gave her or she gave him, slid downward to coil in the hollow at the top of her thighs.

"Oh, dear God," she breathed as he ran his hands down her back to cup her bottom and pull her in closer. She was going up in flames.

"No, it's Liam. Remember that." He skimmed his finger down her cheek, his face so close to hers that she could see a tiny scar crossing one eyebrow. Then he set her on the seat beside him and crossed his arms. "While I'm not a patient man, I have learned self-discipline."

His sudden withdrawal sent a wave of shock vibrating through her. How could he stop when she wanted to straddle his lap and pull his mouth to hers, to cup his hands over her aching breasts and grind herself against his hard thighs until the tension he'd wound inside her released in a glorious explosion?

"So you were playing with me." She tried not to imagine how his lips would feel on her tight nipple.

"I was helping you catch up with the new Liam."

Her body seemed to be catching up faster than her mind. But that created all kinds of other problems. "Now I'm up to date on certain aspects of the new you."

"You used to be a quicker student."

The limousine pulled up to the curb in front of the Bellwether Club. Frankie pulled herself together enough to hit the intercom for the driver. "We should go around to the back so we can use the freight elevator."

Liam gave her an irritated glance. "So I could have bought a bigger tree."

CHAPTER SIX

Within fifteen minutes, the club's staff had delivered the tree and ornaments to her apartment, set the tree up in a stand, and placed a tall stepladder beside it. When the elevator door closed behind the last helper, Frankie looked at Liam as they stood alone in her living room. "Does that answer your question about the competence of my staff?"

"You know I was just twistin' hay to get you out of here."

She nodded. "But it still annoyed me."

"It worked then." He sniffed. "There's something here that smells even better than the tree."

"Irish coffee. On the bar, there."

"*Now* I'm impressed with their competence." He brought the steaming glasses over to the coffee table. "And I see they've swept all the snow off the terrace except the picturesque drifts on the top of the wall. Nice eye they've got."

Frankie sat on the sofa and took a sip of the coffee, feeling the smooth burn of caffeine, cream, and whiskey slide down her throat. "One of the great things about New York is that people here are smart and hardworking. They appreciate training, so they can move up. And except for a few bloody snobs, there's not much class consciousness. Not like in Ireland where you stay in your place or get frozen out. I like it here."

"Yet you had to start your own club."

"I didn't like being judged by someone else's standards. I kept my requirements simple here: one billion dollars that you earned yourself. A high bar but nothing else is necessary."

"High? Some would argue almost impossible."

"The membership is small, but the dues are substantial. And I've never had an uncollectible bill." She smiled over her coffee.

He lounged back on the sofa beside her, stretching out his mile-long legs. "Always the head for money."

"Better than addling my brains by whacking my head into a ball."

He chuckled. "You used to yell, 'There goes calculus' every time I headed the ball. As though I'd ever study higher maths. Did you?"

"No need for it. Accounting, now there's a useful subject."

"I sometimes wish I'd gotten past high school."

"You have other talents," she said. "Besides, a college degree doesn't make you smart. I've hired more than one M.B.A. whom I had to fire six months later."

He frowned into his glass. "I'd have liked to learn some sciences, more about how the world works."

"No one's stopping you from doing it now."

"I don't have time to do homework. I've got a team to whip into shape."

"Well then, after that."

He swallowed down the last of his drink. "It's time to decorate the tree." Tilting his head, he held up his finger for silence so that the faint sound of music could be heard. "Yes, your competent hardworking staff has tuned in to Christmas carols, but we need to turn them up."

"Control, increase volume three levels," Frankie commanded.

The music swelled so the lyrics were distinct.

"Control is a very handy fellow," Liam said. "Where does he live?"

She pointed to a small white panel set into the wall. "Control is the perfect roommate. He doesn't laugh when I listen to ABBA or tell me that the room is too hot when I crank up the temperature on a wintry day."

"But can he hang ornaments on a fir branch?" Liam rose with the perfect control of an athlete at peak fitness. Taking her hand, he pulled her up beside him. "Can Control brush your hair away from your face?" He stroked a loose strand back behind her ear, his fingertips brushing her cheek, her ear, and her neck, starting a ripple of awareness that flowed across her skin.

"Maybe not, but he's damned good at current stock quotes and remembering what movie won best picture in 2001." Her joke couldn't stop the vibration Liam had set loose in her body. It made her want to say to hell with Christmas so she could drag him into her bedroom and strip that too-thick sweater off his hard body.

That was a thought she shouldn't be having.

Liam flipped open a box of ornaments. The sales clerk had thoughtfully provided hooks for the balls. He slipped one on and presented the sphere to Frankie. "You should hang the first and the last."

She looked at the piles of boxes and at the expanse of unadorned green tree. "I vote we go through two boxes and leave the rest to one of my more artistic staff members. Otherwise we'll be here for hours."

Liam put his hands on his hips, drawing her eye to the worn denim pulled taut over his thighs, and surveyed the tree as well. "I'll be casting my vote with yours. That's a hell of a lot of branches."

They started singing along with the carols and then dancing to a few and arguing about why they had chosen that particular ornament. So they'd hung four boxes' worth by the time Frankie threw herself down on the couch, laughing at Liam's hip-swiveling rendition of *All I Want for Christmas is You.* "I'm adding to your nickname. You are now Prince Elvis."

"But I have no intention of leaving the building," he said. "Although I think we should adjourn to the terrace to enjoy the last of the afternoon sunlight."

Frankie inhaled, drawing in the woodsy scent of warmed evergreen. "But it smells so good in here."

"I promise you that it will smell even better as the tree dries out, until you'll feel like you're living in the middle of a pine forest."

"How do you know so much about—" But Liam had disappeared down the hall that led to her bedroom. "Where are you going?"

"To get a blanket." His voice echoed back from the hallway.

When he returned, his arms were filled with the taupe velvet quilt from her bed and a couple of spares that were stored in her linen closet.

"Are you planning to camp out on my terrace?"

"Stow it and follow me."

"*Stow it?*" She should rip into him for such disrespect, but he grinned at her with his eyebrows raised as though daring her to complain. "Ye right bogtrotting maggot of a jackeen."

"That's the Frankie I know and love." He shouldered open the French door and strode to one of the double-wide lounges that stood in the slanting rays of the pale winter sun. Dropping his pile of quilts onto a table, he picked up the top one and draped it over the lounge, then folded the other two at the foot. Sweeping his arm over the well-blanketed chaise, he said, "Join me. Our combined body heat will keep us warm."

There was a hot gleam in his eye that made her pause. She should haul one of the quilts to the lounge next to his. But she wasn't going to. Not after feeling that beautifully muscled body against hers.

She was human, after all.

"Well, if we're just being practical," she said, stretching out on the lounge chair.

Liam came down beside her and pulled the quilts over both of them. The frigid wind still cut through the layers, making Frankie curl into Liam's warmth. "It's perishing out here."

"My nefarious plan worked," he said, slipping his arm under her shoulders and bringing her even closer against him.

As his body heat radiated through her, she let her head rest against his shoulder. The sun struggled to add to the warmth, painting patches of light on the quilt and her cheek. She swiveled her head to see that Liam's hair glowed nearly red while his eyes took on the colors of a still mountain lake. Then his eyelids drifted downward, and he let out a huff of pure contentment. His body seemed to sink deeper into the cushions of the chaise.

"I'm adding a terrace to the list of requirements for an apartment here," he said. His eyes snapped open. "You know what you need? A fire pit."

She couldn't picture herself sitting by a fire pit alone. It was the kind of thing couples did. "Something to ask Santa for."

"You're giving up on world peace?" His eyes were closed again.

Peace was here, sheltered within the strength of Liam's arm, warmed by his big body, lulled by the familiar Irish in his voice. Right now, the rest of the world could go up in flames and she wouldn't care. She wasn't sleepy but she closed her eyes as he did, heightening her other senses. She could hear the occasional snort of a bus or blare of a taxi's horn, but the sounds were muffled here on the back of her expensively private sanctuary. The sharp, chilled air was almost scentless, until she turned her head to inhale Liam, a mixture now of wool, evergreen, and himself, the essence of man and friend and something more that sent an ache of yearning through her.

A helicopter roared overhead, reminding her that the world was still there, would intrude, as he went to work tomorrow, molding his new team into the contenders that would fill all the seats of Yankee Stadium. She would do what she had done twenty-three years ago: send him away for his own good. Back then, it had been to soccer. Now, it would be to find a woman who could give him the family he deserved.

But she wanted a memory to keep with her. Something to fill in the empty spot of the tree when it was taken down after the holidays.

She shifted onto her side and lifted her hand to graze the reddish blond glitter of stubble on his chin, feeling the rasp of it on her fingertips. Although he didn't appear to move, his body somehow pulled tight.

She drew a line along the diagonal of his jaw to the shadow of a cleft in his chin, tracing that shadow up to his bottom lip. When she dragged her finger over the smooth curve of it, she felt his chest rise on a sharp intake of breath.

The strong arcs of his eyebrows gleamed slightly darker than his hair, so she tested the texture of them, softer than she'd expected. His hair tempted her, the thick waving auburn showing a few threads of silver at the temples. Combing her fingers through it so that it fell onto his forehead, she arranged it into a curl before she stroked it back into place again.

"There's more to me than a pretty face," he said, his voice taking on the peaty rasp of a strong whiskey.

She felt a little drunk from it all, as she feathered down the column of his throat and under the quilt, flattening her hand on the middle of his chest. His heart beat hard under her palm but the damned thick sweater once again prevented her from feeling what she wanted. However, she hadn't gotten where she was by letting obstacles stand in her way.

She skimmed her hand down to the sweater's ribbed hem, feeling the buckle of his belt and the denim of his jeans as she slipped her hand under the wool and the cotton tee shirt beneath that. She heard herself make a sound of satisfaction as she found the satin of his bare skin with a glaze of hair in the center. The wall of his abdomen contracted at her touch and he groaned, his breath ruffling through her hair.

"I can't decide if I want to live or die right now," he rumbled.

One hand wasn't enough, so she levered herself up on one elbow, throwing her leg over his. He caught on fast and used his cradling arm to push her up and over to straddle his hips. She felt the ridge of his erection hard underneath her. But she took her time as she skated her palms and fingertips over the rolling contours of his abdomen, inching his sweater higher so she could see as well as touch. His skin was paler here, although she remembered how tan he would get in the summer, even in rainy Ireland, because he and his mates played shirts-and-skins. Despite his reddish hair, he didn't burn, but turned a golden toast. Which was probably why he generally chose the skins side.

"Are the scars from cleats?" She traced a white slash of hard, smooth tissue along his side.

"And surgeries." He twitched as she trailed her fingers along his rib cage. "When you play hard over the years, things stop bending and start to break."

She pushed the sweater higher so that she bared the flat, dusky circles of his nipples. As she put her thumbs to them, feeling the different texture of the darker skin, he hissed in a breath. She glanced down to see his hands clenched around wads of the quilt underneath them. "Are you cold?" she teased.

He let loose a string of Gaelic. Her translation skills were rusty, but it was something to the effect that she was an evil witch sent to drive him out of his several-expletives mind. She laughed and flicked her thumbs over his nipples, now peaked from the cold and her touch.

He released the quilt and grabbed her waist, holding her down against him as he flexed his hips. Her thighs were spread wide over him, so the movement brought the rigid bar of his arousal against the sensitive spot between her legs. Just the one instant of pressure sent an electric streak searing through her, so she arched back without conscious thought, her fingers digging into his chest. The quilt slipped down from her shoulders, but she barely felt the winter air.

He growled and flexed again, making her gasp as her nipples tightened. She braced her hands flat on the slabs of his pecs and rolled her pelvis so she met his movement with hers. Their voices mingled in a wordless chorus of desire.

She started to protest when he released her waist, but then he shoved his hands up under her layers of sweater and shirt to find her breasts, cupping his hard palms over her aching nipples so that she pushed against him as heat rippled and pooled between her legs. A sound of frustration broke from his throat and he skimmed around to the back of her bra to unfasten the hooks with a confident deftness.

His hands were on her bare skin, kneading and tweaking and stroking, so that he focused every nerve in her body on the pleasure his fingers created. She arched and pushed and jerked under his touch as he controlled her like a puppet on strings he held.

"I need to see you. Just for a moment." Before he could get his hands out from under her sweater, she'd yanked it up over her head and tossed it away. The winter air hit her overheated skin like the flat of a chilled steel blade, but the sight of Liam's hands on her breasts and the expression of pure lust on his face sent her blood sizzling through her veins to counteract the cold.

"You're more beautiful than all my fantasies," he said, his touch gone gentle as he grazed his fingertips over one curve and then another.

"Now you." She tugged at his sweater.

He let go of her to bend at the waist, lifting his torso off the chaise with a clench of sheer abdominal muscle power. He jerked his sweater and tee shirt up over his head before he eased back down onto the quilt. The arcs and indentations of his swelling shoulder muscles drew her eyes and her fingers. He was like an ancient warrior carved in marble, except the surface was soft and living and warm.

"You are Cu Chulainn come back to life."

"Why did we wait for this?" he asked, his eyes gone dark and serious as he stroked the back of his hand down her cheek.

She shook her head as though she had no answer. But she did. Somehow she knew their coming together would shift her off balance. A shiver shook her, whether from cold or panic, she wasn't sure.

Liam whipped the quilt up and rolled her under him as though they were back on the sled, except now they were face-to-face. His forearms were braced on either side of her shoulders, but he lowered himself to press his chest lightly against hers, so she could know the size and strength of him enveloping her. "More," she moaned. "Crush me with your body."

More weight came down on her, but she knew he still held himself over her. She opened her thighs so his hips nestled between them and let herself melt under and into him. She fisted her hands in his hair and pulled his head down, opening her mouth to him, inviting him in.

Their tongues touched and challenged and tempted. But it wasn't close to enough. She wanted him moving inside her.

"No more waiting," she said, wedging her hand down between them to push against his erection.

His exhalation whistled past her ear, and he shifted to his side, his face tight with strain and longing. "I wanted it to be on a bed strewn with rose petals by the light of a thousand candles."

"Maybe it's better this way. That we see each other naked by the light of day, clear-eyed and honest." Although she felt at a disadvantage against his well-honed body.

"This time. The first time," he said. "But not always. You don't have to see everything in a harsh light." He leaned in to kiss her with a sweetness that cherished her. And then he seized her shoulders and dragged her up and in, so his mouth could close over the tip of her breast and suck.

The sudden, potent contact on the sensitive skin sent a bolt of arousal to flare between her legs. She managed to yank his belt buckle loose before he took the hint and unfastened his jeans, sitting up in another show of rippling abs to shove them down to his ankles and off, along with his boots and socks. She barely had time to catch a glimpse of a green shape inked low on his hip before he had pulled the quilt back up.

His hands were at her waist, flicking open buckle and button. As he pulled the zipper downward, a powerful attack of shyness shook her. His body showed no trace of age, other than the scars, which only added interest to the balanced interplay of skin, muscle, and sinew. After the early years of making the chocolates herself, a time when her arms showed defined muscles and she stood for hours on end, she'd spent most of her time behind various desks. Now she used the gym at the club, as much to make sure it was up to the standards her members expected as because she enjoyed the exercise. But her stomach had lost the taut flatness of youth, curving ever so gently outwards. She was still proud of the roundness of her bottom, but her thighs showed signs of the effects of gravity and inactivity.

Of course, she'd had lovers over the years, but not recently. Like her billionaires betting on love, she'd become disillusioned with those shallow relationships. She wanted more…or nothing.

But maybe not this much.

"What is it?" Liam's fingers were hooked in the waistband of her jeans, but he did not push them down.

He was too attuned to her moods, even after all these years.

She shook her head. "I'm not as religious about working out as you are."

He closed his eyes and groaned. "I've waited years to touch you like this. Do you think I care if you can bench-press a hundred pounds?"

"But you are so spectacular." She let her gaze travel over the hard muscle of his bare shoulder.

"Well, I won't argue with that." His grin lit up his face. "Now let me show you just how spectacular you are."

He slid down so the quilt covered his head and found her breast with his mouth again. This time he went slowly, laving the tip, licking around the lower swell of it, sliding his teeth gently around the nipple, until he succeeded in making her forget anything other than the hot, wet ache between her legs and her need to have him fill it.

She shoved her jeans down over her hips while he burrowed under the covers to pull off her boots and socks. He kissed his way up the inside of her thigh, using just the moist tip of his tongue to send tingles dancing over her skin. She appreciated his unselfish intentions, but she wanted him *now*. So she twined her fingers into the thick waves of his hair and drew him back up to face her. "I'll take a rain check on that," she said, and kissed him as a thank you. "I need you inside me first."

"We're not rushing this," he said, his breath warm against her lips. He scrabbled around under the quilts before coming up with a condom.

She took it out of his hand. "I don't need this. Do you?"

"Clean as a whistle," he said, his voice barely a rasp.

And then she was on her back, with his beautiful, dear face just over hers. Her thighs were open around his hips and the tip of his cock just touched her.

"Frankie," he said, kissing her eyebrow. "Frankie." He kissed her eyelid. "Frankie." Her temple. "Frankie." The top of her ear.

And she knew why. Because this had taken so long to happen. Because this was the only way they didn't yet know each other.

She bent her knees and opened herself fully to him. He moved into her slowly, so slowly. She held her breath as she felt him easing in, stretching her, filling her. Learning how this felt, how he felt inside her, part of her. No, he'd always been part of her. Would always be part of her. A small, hot tear burned its way out of the corner of her eye, trickling down to sink into the hair at her temple because it was so perfect, this joining.

"*A stór*, am I hurting you?" He stopped moving.

She swallowed hard. "No, no, please, I want all of you."

He gave in to her wish. He was there, deep within her, his weight holding her in place so she could feel the beat of his heart, the breath he sucked in as he went fully in, the vibration in his muscles as he braced himself over her.

"This is where I belong," he said, holding her gaze with his. "Here. Nowhere else."

She curled her hands over his shoulders, loving the solidity of him. For several long moments, they needed nothing more than this connection, this new knowledge of each other. Then, on a long sigh, they both began to move, languidly at first, shifting angles in tiny adjustments to see how they best fit together.

But it was too good. The tension built and tightened inside her, as he slid in and out. She released his shoulders and shifted her hands to dig into the muscular arc of his backside, tilting her hips to urge him on. He straightened his arms, raising himself up to drive into her faster and harder. "Yes, yes, yes!" She moved with him to bring him in deeper.

He thrust in and ground his hips against her. For what seemed like an eternity, she balanced on the edge of her climax, every molecule of her body pulling in to her core before it all exploded outward like a supernova, sending her arching up and back as her muscles clenched and released, clenched and released.

"Frankie, *a rúnsearc!*" Liam bowed back and shouted as he pushed into her again. And she felt the liquid of his release, the pulse of his cock, sending another orgasm tearing through her.

He stayed, holding her in place with his weight, while the throb of his cock and the aftershocks of her climax gentled and subsided. At last, he let his arms bend, settling over her and then bringing them both onto their sides as he slipped out of her.

He cradled her against his chest, tucking the rumpled quilts back around her. His heart was pounding against her ear, proving that he had been as affected as she was. She curled her hands in between herself and Liam, wanting to crawl inside him to hold onto the intimacy as long as possible.

She drifted, remembering moments and sensations, her body floating down from the high of their climax. The Gaelic he'd shouted as he came echoed through her mind. *A rúnsearc. My secret beloved,* the most passionate of endearments. She pushed it away. If it had been wrung from him simply by the power of their orgasm, she didn't want to know it. If he'd meant it, that was even worse.

No, she would allow herself this day, this night, to be together with him in every way. Tomorrow would come soon enough.

The sun had sunk low enough on the horizon that the surrounding buildings cast shadows over her terrace. She shivered. "As hot as you are in every way, it's too cold to stay out here without clothes," she said.

"You must be hotter than I am because I wasn't noticing the chill at all." He ran his hand down her back to squeeze her bottom. "Let's get you bundled up for the trip inside."

He separated one quilt from the tangled pile and wrapped it around her. "You dash and I'll grab our clothes on the way."

She was about to say that she could handle her own clothes. But something stopped her. Something that whispered it would be nice to let another person take care of her for a moment. He wasn't cold—he'd said so—so why be bullheaded about pulling her weight? "See you inside!"

She bolted for the French doors, the soles of her bare feet burning with cold by the time she'd gotten across the frigid tiles of the terrace floor. Slipping inside, she went straight to the fireplace to hold her feet out one at a time to the flames.

Liam burst through the door, his arms full of quilts, clothes, and boots. "Jaysus, it'd freeze the bollocks off a polar bear out there."

He dumped his burdens, including the quilt that had been draped over his shoulders, on a chair and strode toward Frankie and the fire, in all his naked, muscle-rippling glory. She didn't pretend not to ogle him every step of the way, and once again she caught the flash of a green tattoo on his hip.

"You have to pay for looking." He grinned as he took one corner of her quilt out of her hand, and wrapped it around his big body.

As he huddled in beside her, his chilled skin grazed hers. She yelped. "'Tis like diving into the bloody Irish Sea in January."

"You'll warm me up fast." He snaked his arm around her waist to pull her into him. She let her eyes close as their skin pressed together, savoring the contrast of his hard contours against her softer curves, the delight of it quickly warding off the shock of that first contact.

"Liam, what's the tattoo on your hip?"

CHAPTER SEVEN

Liam had forgotten about the damned tattoo. It was so much a part of him, he never gave it a thought. But he knew Frankie. She would lock those laser-focused eyes on it the first time she got a chance and ask the question he didn't want to have to answer just yet.

He couldn't lie to her, though.

He willed himself not to tense up. "It's a shamrock, of course."

"When did you get it?"

That was easy. "My first year at football…soccer academy. The ink was a statement of my ambition to make Team Ireland."

"Is there only the one?"

It was all one image, just added to over time. "One tattoo. My coach was pissed enough about that one. He told me my body was a fine instrument, not a canvas for amateur artwork."

"Good God, what would he say about David Beckham?"

"It would blister your ears off, for certain. But he's passed on, so he's not obliged to comment on Becks' body art." He'd skated past that one, but just barely.

"I'm sorry. I can tell you liked him." She stood on tiptoe to kiss his cheek.

He put his other arm around her and held her there against his chest. "You could tell I liked him from two sentences. And you wonder why I tracked you down."

Frankie raised her eyebrows at him. "You sound like a bloodhound."

He laughed. "Always the romantic."

She was so small in his arms. And soft. Frankie, soft. She'd always seemed more like a fire-tempered rapier, flexible but razor-sharp, slicing through anything that got in her way. But she'd opened herself to him, given herself with a generosity and lack of reserve he hadn't considered dreaming of. Her body had seared itself into his mind, into his skin, into his soul.

And he knew he had to fight for this with everything he had.

The heat from the fire soaked through the quilt, and he felt the beginning of sweat sheening his skin and hers. "How about we finish decorating the tree?"

"Nude?" She sounded intrigued, not shocked. She reached down and ran her palm over his cock, making it swell with pleasure. "Can I hang an ornament here?"

"They don't make a hook big enough," he said, running through his new team's roster in his head to keep himself under control.

She chuckled, and stroked down the length of him again. He clenched his jaw to keep from groaning out the lust her touch sent torching through him.

"Let's go to bed then," she said, before giving him a heavy-lidded look and faking a yawn. "I find I'm exhausted from all the exercise and fresh air."

When Frankie went after something, she never did it by halves. "You're not fooling me with the yawn, woman. You're after my elite athlete's body, you are."

"And are you complaining?" She ran her hand over his cock yet again, making it pull tighter.

"Well, one part of my body isn't." But he knew she would find the tattoo, and he would have to give her an explanation.

"That's the only part that matters for my purposes." Somehow she whipped the quilt away from him, so it was wrapped only around her. "Go ahead of me to the bedroom," she said, her eyes lit by a lascivious gleam.

"So you can ogle my bum?"

"I'm going to ogle every inch of you," she said.

"In that case." He turned and sauntered toward the hallway.

He heard her sigh. "I love the way your muscles move under your skin. Like a Thoroughbred racehorse. All that power and grace."

"I'm not sure I like being compared to an animal." But her words made his cock rise higher. He could feel her gaze like a brush of fingers over the skin of his back.

"Not even to a stud?"

"Ah, when you put it that way." He stepped through her bedroom door and turned to catch her and snatch the quilt away from around her. "Now, you have to walk in front of me to the bed."

He watched in shock as a tint of pink flushed her cheeks. "Are you blushing?"

She lifted her chin but didn't quite meet his gaze. "I'm forty-nine years old. And not an athlete."

He couldn't believe it. Running his hands down from her shoulders to her hands to hold them out from her sides, he let his eyes skim over the fullness of her breasts, the curve of her belly, and lower. The reaction of his cock was unmistakable. "Frankie, you are the most beautiful woman I've ever seen."

She shook her head. "You're blind, but I'll walk to the bed for you because you blarneyed me into it."

Frustration wedged in his chest. "It's not blarney, ye gobdaw. And I'll prove it to you."

He turned her and gave her a nudge toward the big bed with its snow-white sheets exposed by the lack of the quilt he'd stolen from it. Being Frankie, she strode toward it with her head up and her shoulders back. Then she pulled the sheet back and climbed under it.

"No, *a stór*, no covering that gorgeous body. I want to worship it." He tugged the sheet down to her feet and began there, massaging her high, strong arches, kissing the bone on the inside of her ankle, inhaling the scent of woman and evergreen and a whiff of arousal. But something was missing. He looked up to find her watching him through half-closed eyes.

"You don't smell of chocolate anymore," he said.

"Do you miss it?"

"It was part of you."

"I'll rub some candy bars on my skin next time."

"No, I will. Melted candy bars. Then I'll lick the chocolate off you." He heard the hiss of her breath being sucked in.

Then he told her, in detail, where he would rub the candy bars as he kissed each place. And he told her, in detail, how lovely all those places were. The curve of her calves. The back of her knees. The soft skin inside her thighs. The convexity of her belly. The swell of her hips. Oh, dear God, everything about her breasts. The line of her clavicle. The vulnerable hollow at the base of her throat. The sensitive spot just behind her ears.

She was moaning and twisting and clutching at the sheets and at him before he skimmed his lips down the center of her torso, dipped his tongue into her navel, and then moved lower. He found the exquisite wet pinkness between her legs and licked, adding his moans to hers as he tasted the salt and musk of her. Her fingers combed through his hair and then held there. She opened her legs and let him suck and plunge and revel in the liquid heat of her response. When he slid two fingers inside her, she arched up and shouted his name as her inner muscles slammed closed and open, so that he could feel the pressure and the moisture of her release. He used his tongue and his hand to keep her orgasm going until she begged him to stop. "It's too much," she gasped. "I can't…."

As he slipped his fingers out, her muscles clenched again. "You did," he said.

He lifted his fingers to inhale the aroma of her, rubbed them against his tongue to savor the taste of her. Kneeling between her sprawled legs, he let his gaze roam over the delicious curves he was beginning to know intimately, the sexual flush on her creamy skin, the spread of her silver hair over the sheets. Her soft lips were parted and her chest heaved as she drew in deep breaths while she came down from her climax. He brought his fingers to his nostrils again, pulling her scent in so that it seemed to ripple down to wrap around his erect cock.

She opened her eyes. "That was worth waiting twenty-three years for."

He threw back his head and laughed, letting a tension he'd been carrying for a long time spill out of his mouth. He knew he was a deft lover. Enough women had told him so. But this was Frankie, and he'd wanted it to be perfect for her.

"And I see that you're still waiting," she said, her gaze dropping to the erection rising from between his thighs.

"I can wait a wee bit longer," he said, circling his fingers around one of her ankles to bend her leg so he could roll her and stretch out beside her, his cock snugged between the cheeks of her bottom. He could easily come just by rubbing himself against the ripe roundness there.

As though reading his mind, she shifted backwards to nestle him closer in.

"You're killing me, Frankie."

"Just keeping your interest up until I can return the favor."

He slipped a hand around to cup the velvety weight of her breast. "This will help."

"Ah, but whose interest are you keeping up now?" she asked, pushing her tight nipple into his palm.

The hard press of her on his skin nearly undid him, but he held onto his control. He could feel tiny shudders still running through her body, and smiled with satisfaction. Then a fist of emotions, so many he couldn't name them all, lodged in his throat as he enfolded her small, strong body in his arms. The touch of her skin against his thighs, his belly, his chest. Her heat radiating through him. The sound of her breathing, the thud of her pulse, the silky brush of her hair. His dreams had not prepared him for the sweetness of the reality and it nearly overwhelmed him. He swallowed, his eyelids squeezed closed against a burn of tears.

She was right. It was too much.

"Liam, could you ease up a bit so my ribs stay intact?"

He loosened the grip he'd unconsciously tightened. "Just making sure you don't slip away from me again."

Her body jerked a little and she sighed. "You knew I wasn't going to stay in Finglas."

"I didn't mean it that way." He released her breast to smooth his hand over her hair. "I've imagined this for so long that I can't believe it's real and not a leprechaun's trick."

She wriggled against his erection. "Feels solid as a rock to me."

He moaned at the blast of sensation. Frankie levered herself up to kneel beside him. Putting her hand on his shoulder, she pushed him onto his back. "I could just look at you forever," she said, her gaze traveling down and up again, making his cock twitch as though she'd touched it. "I lied," she said, resting her hands on his chest. "I need to touch you."

She leaned over, her hair brushing his skin, and kissed first one of his flat nipples and then the other. Her touch ricocheted down to his groin, drawing it tighter. His bollocks were aching. "Frankie, do you mean to drive me out of my bloody mind?"

She laughed against his skin, making his hips flex without his willing them to. Then she trailed her lips down the center of his body, the silkiness of her hair dragging over his skin, slowing as she got closer to the place he wanted her mouth. She traced her tongue along the defined line that ran from his hip to his groin. He held his breath and watched as she braced one hand on the bed beside him and raised the other to feather it across the head of his cock. And then he was lost, swamped by the feel of her fingers, her mouth, her tongue on his straining, yearning skin.

He came with a blast of pleasure, wringing out every muscle and every nerve, emptying him of all thought except Frankie.

When he could open his eyes again, she was sitting back on her heels, a smug smile curling her lips. "You're a loud one, Keller."

"Did I say something? My mind was obliterated by a nuclear explosion."

She laughed once. "A man's mind is an easy thing to turn blank with sex."

It hurt him that she thought of it as nothing more than sex, but he wasn't going to call her out on it yet. She could get mulish when pushed.

She crawled up the bed and fitted herself against his side, her head pillowed on his shoulder. Her fingers drifted over his chest and ribs and then down to his hip, tracing the shamrock inked there. "Tell me what the 'O' and the 'F' stand for."

He felt as though she'd slammed her fist into his gut. Dragging in a breath, he forced his voice to sound relaxed. "Can't you guess about the 'F'?"

"Not without sounding conceited beyond belief."

He tried to laugh, but his throat wouldn't release enough. "Of course it's for you, ye eejit. I wouldn't defile my body for anyone else."

"But you did. The 'O'." She said it softly.

He brought his hand over to cover hers, flattening it over the tattoo. "The only other person in the world I love as much as I do you." He drew in another breath. "Owen. My son."

Joy roared through Frankie, squeezing tears from her eyes. She'd always hoped that he would be a father. The kids in Finglas had followed him around as though he were the Pied Piper. Unlike most of the older boys, he wasn't too proud to play soccer with the younger ones, giving them tips on their game. There was so little kindness in their world that it tugged at her heart to watch him on the soccer pitch with the wee ones swarming around him.

"Why are you crying, Frankie?" His voice was tight with some strain she couldn't interpret and his hand nearly crushed hers against the point of his hip.

She lifted her head to let him see her happiness and found him scowling. "Because you were meant to be a father. He's a lucky boy, your Owen."

His face relaxed as Liam closed his eyes and then opened them again. "You scared the shite out of me. I thought you.... But you're crying."

"Because I'm happy for you." She'd cried more in the last two days than in the last five years. "But there hasn't been a breath of it in the press. How did you keep it a secret?"

Liam wrapped his arm around her shoulders and hitched them both up to sit against the headboard. "There are always ways to avoid the press. And deals to be made with them when you can't." His voice went hard on the last. "He lives in New Jersey, so I didn't get to visit him often."

"And his mother? I won't ask you if you're married to her because you wouldn't be here if you were."

He sighed. "Ten years ago I had a weekend fling with a friend of a friend that had unexpected consequences. We were both careful but...things happen." He shook his head. "Neither of us wanted an abortion, but we also didn't want a wedding. So I provided the money, and she made a good home for Owen."

She heard the satisfaction in Liam's voice that he'd been able to give his son the things he'd longed for as a child. "Is that why you took the job here?" she asked.

"Two reasons. Owen and you."

The strength of her desire to see Liam's son shocked her, but she didn't want to mislead Liam into believing that would change anything between them. "Do you have a picture of him?"

"On my phone, which is somewhere in the heap of clothes in your living room." His grip on her gentled and she felt his lips against her hair. "*A stór,* you and Owen are kindred spirits."

"I can't imagine a ten-year-old boy being a coldhearted cynic."

She felt him tense. "That's just the facade. I know the generous, caring woman behind it."

"Dear God, don't spew that mush to anyone else. It will ruin my reputation." But his words spread warmth in her chest.

"Tough as nails Frankie." His tone was so tender and understanding that she wanted to curl into him. "But that's not what you and Owen have in common. It's that he likes to blow things up."

"I don't recall ever joining the IRA." She made her tone dry.

"He's a chemist. He stirs things together to see what happens. Like you and your chocolate." He picked up her hand and kissed one of the burn scars made by a spill of melted chocolate. "You have more of these than when I knew you."

"You can't avoid them when you're cooking."

He kissed another one on her wrist and sighed, his breath feathering over her skin deliciously. "I imagine Owen will collect similar marks. His mother says he's obsessed."

"More important, how's his corner kick?"

Liam's muscles tensed under her again. "He has no interest in sports."

She saw the bafflement in his face. "Did his mother steer him away from them?"

"No, Carolyn plays tennis and rides horses." He shrugged. "Owen will have a kickabout with me but he's just being polite to his da."

"And you don't know what to do with him." Her heart squeezed with sadness for Liam. How could he have a son who didn't want to play ball with him?

His face was bleak as he said, "Soccer's been my whole life."

"So go to a science museum with him, and let Owen expand your horizons. That will be exciting for him." Now she understood why Liam had been thinking about studying the sciences.

"For someone who says she doesn't like kids, you have some smart ideas about them."

"I figure kids are just people on a smaller scale. People love to share their expertise. It's showing off, but in a constructive way." For all her siblings, she knew almost nothing about relating to a child on any but the most basic level of caretaking.

"So you'll meet him and let him show you how to blow things up?" He stroked her shoulder.

"You keep trapping me with my own words."

"There's no other way to do it."

CHAPTER EIGHT

Frankie pulled on a sweater in a soft rose color and inspected the effect in the mirror. She shook her head and whipped it off, tossing it onto the multi-colored pile on her bed.

Catching sight of her bare torso in the reflection, she ran her hands over the curve of her lace-covered breasts before skimming her palms down over her hips. These were just a few of the places Liam had touched and kissed and murmured passionate compliments about these last two nights. Her body simmered with a contented warmth that flared into blazing desire whenever Liam came near.

But the thought of meeting his son turned desire into nerves.

"He's a ten-year-old boy. He doesn't give a damn what I wear," she growled as she surveyed the jumbled array.

Pulling a white silk blouse and navy blue cashmere sweater out of the mess, she shrugged into them. Paired with gray wool trousers and high-heeled black pumps, this was a casual look she was comfortable in.

"Good enough."

She checked her watch. Owen had a half day of school before his Christmas vacation began, so she and Liam were picking him up to go out for lunch. Frankie checked the shopping bag that held the gifts she'd bought for Owen: a food chemistry set and a Taste of Ireland chocolate sampler.

She smoothed her hair, grabbed her jacket, and strode to her private elevator. As she reached it, the doors slid open and Liam stepped out. He wore jeans that hugged every muscle in his thighs and a quarter-zip gray pullover in some stretchy athletic material that did the same favor for the swell of his wide shoulders.

"You didn't have to come up," Frankie said, lifting her face to meet his kiss.

Their lips touched, touched again, and then his arms were around her, his fingers twined in her hair. After he'd sent waves of heat rippling through her, he pulled away. "You draw me like a magnet, Frankie."

With a sigh, she brushed back the hair that had fallen over his forehead. She should stop this now, but her usual steely discipline had deserted her. "That's the attraction of opposites. We're too alike for that."

"Male and female. Hard and soft. I find all the differences I need." His hands drifted down her back to cup the curves of her behind before he gave her a light smack and released her. "We'd better go. Traffic to New Jersey can be a right bastard."

The playful gesture shocked her before a strange sadness wound through her. No one ever touched her with that kind of casual familiarity.

He took the shopping bag from her. "What's this?"

"Gifts for Owen."

"He's already got piles of presents around the Christmas tree."

Frankie looked him in the eye. "I know the effectiveness of a well-placed bribe."

He chuckled and waved her into the elevator.

As the car glided downwards, the air in it vibrated with an odd tension. Frankie slid a sideways glance toward Liam's profile and saw that his jaw was tight and his lips had lost any curve of a smile.

"What is it, Prince?"

He shook his head, making the lock of hair curve onto his forehead again. Before she could probe further, the elevator door opened, and he swept her out to the limousine waiting in front.

When they were settled in the back, he interlaced his fingers with hers and fixed his gaze straight ahead. "Carolyn's engaged to be married. She just told me."

His grip tightened.

She put her hand flat against his cheek and rotated his head toward her so their eyes met. "You will still be his father."

But she understood that the new stepfather would have the advantage of being with the boy every day, a constant presence in his life. While Liam was just a visitor, no matter how glamorous he was.

He turned to kiss her palm and looked away again. "I've met him. He's, well, he's the kind of man you'd choose for a boy to have as a father."

"You wouldn't want any other kind for Owen."

"I know." His voice was like gravel. Her heart wept for him.

"You're Liam Keller, international soccer superstar, coach of a major New York team, media darling. His friends—and their fathers—will beg to meet you."

"I don't want to be some sort of status symbol. I want to be his da."

"So you buy a house nearby. You negotiate a schedule with Carolyn. You take him to school some days. You pick him up from school some days. You get some holidays with him. And Owen will be a lucky boy to have two men in his life who are great role models and who love him. It's a hell of a lot more than you and I ever had."

Liam nodded and she saw some of the tension leave his face. "You always knew how to kick me in the arse when I was acting the maggot."

"You aren't acting the maggot. You're being a father." And she wanted to take the hurt away from him. "Does Owen know about the engagement?"

Liam shook his head. "He knows Don and his mom spend a lot of time together."

"I'm sure he hopes you and Carolyn will get together. That's what children do." She hesitated a moment before asking, "Did you and Carolyn consider marrying?"

"We did, but we barely knew each other." He blew out a long breath. "As we spent time together, she felt she deserved better."

"She must be a gobshite of the first order if she thinks she could find a better man than you." Frankie had an overwhelming urge to smack sense into a woman she'd never met.

Liam gave her a long, level look. "She deserved better than a man who's in love with another woman."

Frankie felt as though he'd slammed her back against the seat, but she concentrated on not moving a muscle. "You told her that."

"I'm not an eejit. She figured it out on her own."

Her stomach plunged like an airplane caught in a downdraft. She'd dismissed all his declarations of undying love as exaggerations, meant to blarney her into his arms. But Carolyn had seen the reality of his feelings.

"I'm sorry," she said, stalling to give herself time to wrestle her own response under control. Because her heart had soared back up and hurled itself against the walls of her chest, trying to force her to tell Liam that she loved him too. Always had.

Always would.

"I'm not," he said.

Her heart slammed into her rib cage again. Maybe the age difference no longer mattered. Maybe his athletic success could counterbalance her enormous wealth. Maybe Owen would be enough of a family for him.

Too many maybes. She'd never go into a business deal with all those unknowns.

Liam leaned against the door of the limo, scanning the crowd of children pouring out of the brick school building's double doors. Frankie had elected to stay in the car, claiming Owen needed to know he was the focus of Liam's attention.

She'd changed the subject after he'd told her about Carolyn. And he'd let her do it because he was afraid to push any harder. Frankie had built so many walls between them. He wasn't sure he could tear them all down. And the thought of her walking away again shredded his guts.

"Da!" Owen's young voice yanked him out of his unhappy thoughts. The boy was barreling down the front sidewalk, his backpack bouncing behind him as he waved a square of brown paper in the air.

Liam's chest squeezed as it always did when he saw his son's face light up at the sight of him. In two strides he was across the street and kneeling to catch Owen in his arms, the boy's thin shoulders feeling as light and fragile as a bird's under his hands.

"Look at the cool picture frame I made you. It's a reindeer," Owen said, leaning back against Liam's embrace to hold out the construction paper frame decorated with antlers on the top, two plastic eyes on the sides, and a button nose on the bottom. "It's a little babyish because the teacher made us outline our hands for the antlers, but the moving eyes are cool. Mom said I could give it to you because she got the snowman snow globe."

"Your mom's a generous lady to give up such a magnificent gift," Liam said, working to keep his voice steady as he touched one hand-shaped antler. He still had every paper, painting, and craft project that Owen or Carolyn had given him. "I'll need a picture of you to put in it, and then I'll display it on my coffee table for everyone to admire."

"Maybe we could take a picture with you in it too," Owen said, with a shy sideways glance.

Liam wanted to squeeze Owen in a bear hug for that. "That would be even better. I've got a friend with me who could take that photo for us."

The light in his son's face dimmed. "It's not just us?"

"It's my old friend, Frankie. I've told you stories about her."

Owen perked up. "The chocolate lady?"

Liam nodded and rose, taking Owen's hand to walk to the limo. A couple of parents nodded to Liam with recognition written on their faces. Several of Owen's classmates wished him happy holidays.

"Let me have your backpack and then you can scoot in beside Frankie," Liam said, before he slid onto the leather seat beside his son. "Frankie, meet Owen. Owen, you've heard a lot about Frankie."

Surprise showed in the slight lift of Frankie's eyebrows, but she held out her hand. "Nice to meet you, Owen. I've known your dad for a long time."

Owen put his small hand in hers. "Nice to meet you too. Da says your chocolates are the best in the world."

"Maybe you should find out for yourself. I brought some with me."

Owen's eyes went wide as Frankie pulled the sizeable Taste of Ireland sampler out of her shopping bag. "Da's given me some before, but never this much." He turned to Liam. "Can I have one before lunch? I'm so *hungry*."

Frankie flinched before she could stop herself, as the child's voice hurled her back into the bedroom she shared with her sisters. She forced herself to breathe through the sudden clutch of panic.

"It's a special occasion, so I think it can be allowed," Liam said, his smile fading into a look of puzzled concern as he scanned Frankie's face.

It had been hard enough to keep herself in the present when she saw Owen through the car window. Except for the child's mop of dark blond hair, he was the spitting image of Liam as a boy with the same wiry body and coiled energy. When the boy had slipped into the car and turned Liam's dark blue eyes on her, she'd nearly gasped.

Owen ripped the plastic off the box of chocolates and lifted off the top, giving Frankie time to fight down the memories of other small, but thinner hands, reaching for the occasional rejected chocolate she brought home from work at Balfour's. Owen started to pick out a Minty Shamrock before pulling back and holding the box out to her. "Would you like one?"

"You're a very polite young man, but they're all yours. Are Minty Shamrocks your favorite?"

Owen took the shamrock before offering the box to his father. "I like the way the shape feels on my tongue before I bite into it and let the mint out." He popped the chocolate into his mouth.

"A real connoisseur." Frankie was impressed with the sophistication of his answer. "I think you'll like this other gift then." She pulled the chemistry kit from the shopping bag.

"Don't I have to wait until Christmas to open it?" But Owen had already plunked the box of chocolates down on his father's lap.

"It's not wrapped in Christmas paper, so that eliminates the need to wait." She transferred the large box to Owen.

"You're cool," the boy said, as he found a corner of the brown wrapping paper and pulled.

The pleasure on Liam's face made Frankie's heart twist with sadness. She could almost feel the power of his longing to have his son and his oldest friend take to each other.

Owen ripped the wrapping off the front of the box. "This is *awesome*! Is there chocolate in it?"

Frankie pointed to the chocolate wafers in the photo on the box. "But I'll send you more since you have such a fine palate for it."

"I do?"

"That means you don't just know that the chocolate tastes good, you know *why* it tastes that way," Frankie said.

"I have a fine palate," Owen said to his father.

Liam ruffled the boy's hair. "And she would know because she's a professional."

The limousine came to a stop by the curb. Owen leaned over Frankie to look out the window. "It's Paddy's Pub," he said, his young voice vibrating with excitement.

"A pub?" Frankie had made too many trips to the neighborhood pub in Finglas to collect her father when he was too drunk to find his own way home.

"One of my mates from Team Ireland owns it, so Owen gets treated like visiting royalty," Liam said, before he added in a low voice, "and it's nothing like the Leprechaun."

Her father's favorite boozer to get plastered in. "Thank God."

"They have the best chips in America," Owen said. "Paddy's secret recipe."

The limo driver swung open the door and offered his hand to Frankie while Owen scrambled out behind her. Frankie eyed the half-timbered facade with mullioned windows and a bright green shamrock painted on the faux-Tudor sign. "Just like the Auld Sod," she said, her tone as dry as desert sand. But relief loosened the clench of her shoulders. Liam was right. It was nothing like the Leprechaun.

"Americans like the atmosphere, according to Paddy," Liam said. Owen was already at the door, looking over his shoulder at them. Liam held out his hand to Frankie. She took it, knowing he meant it to be a comfort to her. She regretted it when she saw the boy's smile fade as he saw his father's gesture.

Liam drew her forward and held the door open. Frankie waved Owen through in front of her, and the air exploded with a chorus of Irish accents shouting, "Owen! Liam!" followed by various abusively friendly greetings.

The interior continued the ye-olde-historic-pub theme with dark paneling, a long polished bar, dart boards, and brass lamps, all serving as a background for a shrine to Irish football. She couldn't call it soccer here where photos, posters, framed jerseys, and scarves were all tributes to Team Ireland.

The din of welcome quieted to a single voice, as a blond man of about Liam's age came toward them with his hand thrust out. He wore jeans and a button-down shirt striped in green and orange. His stride was fluid and efficient, reminding her of Liam's. This must be his former teammate.

"Paddy Naughton," the man said, taking her hand. "You're much too lovely a lass to be hangin' around the likes of Liam Keller, so I'll be glad to rescue you."

She put her hand in his warm, strong grasp. "Frankie Hogan." It came out in full-on Irish, an involuntary response to Paddy's deep accent.

"Ye're a Dubliner, then. That deserves a kiss." He leaned in to give her a smacking buss on the cheek.

"Away and pull yer wire," Liam said, putting his arm around Frankie's waist.

Paddy winked at her. "Don't go actin' the maggot, Kells. I was just bein' cordial."

Owen was already perched on a stool, chatting with the bartender. Liam tapped his son on the shoulder. "We'll be taking a table today."

The boy sighed but jumped off the stool and followed them to a high-backed booth. Paddy handed Frankie a menu and nodded to the wall beside her. "Thought you'd appreciate the Liam Keller table."

She looked up and saw the photograph of Liam sitting on his teammates' shoulders, his head thrown back in a silent shout as he lifted his arms above his head. His hair was matted to his skull and his knees were bloody, but his face was lit with the savage joy of triumph. She had the same photograph in the file in her office. It was from the game that had advanced Ireland to the quarter-finals of the World Cup. And one of her favorites because it showed the essence of the boy who wouldn't allow the world to beat him down.

"Can we order food now?" Owen asked. "I'm *starving.*"

His child's whine slashed through her, and all the memories, all the images, all the Irishness of this place swelled up in her chest until she couldn't breathe, couldn't see, couldn't slow the pounding of her heart.

Sweat seemed to erupt from her pores, soaking her blouse so it clung to her skin as she saw her six-year-old sister double over, sobbing and clutching her stomach when the hunger cramps grew too strong. The disappointed faces of her younger siblings arrayed around the table as she dished out one spoonful of watery boiled potatoes on each plate and nothing more. The humiliation of coaching her youngest sister to open her big blue eyes wide when Frankie took her to the grocer's to beg for rotten fruit.

She was going to explode.

"Liam, I'm not feeling well. I'll wait in the car." She brushed away his concern as he rose to let her scramble out of the booth. Calling on every ounce of strength she could muster, she locked her eyes on his and spoke in a normal tone, "Stay with Owen. I need air, that's all."

She bolted out the door and into the car. Dropping her head back against the seat, she forced herself to breathe in for six seconds, hold for six seconds, breathe out for six seconds. The child's cry

I'm starving beat against the inside of her skull like a hammer against a gong.

She yanked out her phone. "Vincent, I need to get back there ASAP. Send a car and the chopper."

By the time Liam had gotten Owen's lunch to go and dragged his son to the limo, Frankie was gone. The driver said a car had picked her up not five minutes after she'd made a phone call. "She asked me to give you these," he said, handing Liam two small folded notes.

He flipped open the one with his name on it.

> *Dear Liam,*
> *Your son is a fine young man. You should be very proud of him. I am honored that I got to meet him. But it's too much. All the memories. I can't. I'm sorry.*
>
> *Frankie*

He crumpled the paper with a snarl. She couldn't even bring herself to add a word of affection in her closing.

"Da? What happened to Frankie?" Owen asked.

Liam shoved the balled-up paper into his pocket. "She got sick and went home."

"But the limo's still here."

"She's a very resourceful lady, so she called a cab." Or something faster, to carry her away from her past. "Here's your lunch. Go ahead and eat in the car."

Owen grabbed the takeout bag with enthusiasm, while Liam unfolded the note with Owen's name on it. He wasn't handing his son anything that Frankie had written without checking it first.

> *Dear Owen,*
>
> *I'm sorry to leave without saying good-bye. I might have a touch of the stomach flu, and I didn't want to pass my germs to you and your da. I've known your da for a long, long time, and I want to tell you that he is the strongest, most honorable man I've ever met. You can always trust him to have your back, to take care of you, to be there when you need him. He will love you truly, with everything in him. And he will never hurt you. You are too young to understand what a rare thing that is, but in time you will. Be good to him, Owen, and love him with all your heart. He is one of the few people who is worthy of it.*
>
> *Warmest regards,*
> *Frankie*

Liam folded the note as though it were fine, fragile silk, smoothing it between his fingers. He stood with his head down while he fought back the black sea of anguish trying to drown him. Maybe he would give Owen this note one day, but not now.

These could be the last words he would ever have from Frankie.

CHAPTER NINE

Frankie stepped out of her elevator and walked straight to the door to her terrace. She needed the slap and bite of the frigid winter wind to counter the storm raging in her mind and heart. She walked to the wall and pressed her hands down into the frosting of snow Liam had joked about her staff leaving for picturesque effect.

Liam. Her body jerked as though she'd been shocked. She threw her head back as she fought the torrent of agony the thought of him sent roaring through her. A long, low moan wrenched itself from her throat, rising to the gunmetal gray sky.

She felt as though some part of her, an organ deep inside her body, had been cut out of her, leaving a gaping emptiness that was worse than the slash of a razor blade. She'd carried him there, next to her heart, all these years. And now she had to rip him out because her past could still rise up and destroy her.

Her hands burned with cold, but she held them against the snow and frozen stone, pushing them against the gritty surface.

She wasn't strong enough to face down her terrors and come to Liam as a whole, undamaged person. She wasn't worthy of his love, wasn't worthy even to claim his friendship.

The wind sliced through her thin cashmere sweater and she shuddered. Frostbite and pneumonia weren't the answer, so she tucked her hands under her arms and trudged back into the warmth of her apartment. Her gaze went to the framed photos Liam had picked up. The ones she'd carried with her everywhere.

Walking straight to them, she picked up the frame and flipped open the back to pull the strip of paper out. She touched the two young faces, the excitement of their smiles contrasting with the fear and loneliness in their eyes. The soccer academy was Liam's big chance, and they both burned for him to succeed.

But they'd survived the desperation and dangers of Finglas because they'd always had each other. Once he left, there had been no one to cheer her on, no one to trust with her secrets, no one to protect her from her mistakes.

She hadn't cried that day, not even after Liam's ferry to England had rumbled away from the dock. She'd gone to work and wrapped herself in the warm, comforting aroma of melted chocolate.

Now tears streaked down her cheeks, one after the other, dropping onto the two tiny photos, making the cheap chemicals fade. She let them.

Carrying the small photos with her, she went to her bedroom and took the two enlargements off the wall. She ripped off the backing and pulled the two pictures out of the frames before she headed back to the elevator.

When it opened on the first floor, she strode to her office suite, closing the door to the reception area before she walked to the fireplace. As always in the winter, a small fire flickered there. She tilted the metal fire screen forward and flicked the photos into the flames, watching them curl and turn black around the edges before they burned.

As soon as the last ash dropped through the grate, she retrieved the key to her office safe and pulled the massive door open. The leather file box that held all the clippings and photos of Liam that she'd collected over the years stood on a shelf, right at eye level. She yanked it out and carried it to her desk, sitting down to lift off the lid.

She pulled the most recent folder out. It was filled with stories and photos announcing that Liam had signed on as head coach for the New York Challenge, the city's new, high profile soccer team, created by the same organization that owned the New York Yankees. She flipped it open to be hit by a head shot of Liam looking directly into the camera with a confident smile on his face, just like the one he'd worn as he surveyed the vast emptiness of

Yankee Stadium the night of their dinner there. She slumped back in her chair and closed her eyes until the anguish lessened enough for her to breathe again.

Swiveling, she fed the folder into the high-powered paper shredder, wincing as the razor-sharp blades chewed through the papers she'd pored over when she craved the sight of her old friend.

The next folder was a little easier to handle because it covered the time Liam spent coaching in Europe. There were fewer photos and they were older. It went into the shredder before the blades had finished destroying the first one.

When she reached the folder covering Liam's years on Team Ireland, she couldn't stop herself from turning over each article and photo. They were arranged in reverse chronological order by the service she paid to track every mention of Liam Keller. There was the photo Paddy's Pub had on their wall, but the one she loved best was of his debut on the team, when he'd scored his first goal for Ireland on a penalty kick. The camera had captured the moment he'd fallen to his knees, his head thrown back and his eyes closed. She knew he wasn't praying because neither of them had believed in heavenly intervention, so she'd always assumed he was imprinting the moment on his memory.

As she took one last look at the picture, she drew in her breath on a gasp. She'd never noticed before that one of his hands rested on his hip but not in the typical location. It was just enough lower to look odd. She dropped the folder on the desk and grabbed the computer mouse to open the file of game videos. The service had edited them to highlight Liam's position on the field. She clicked on a different game where she knew he had taken a penalty kick.

The camera followed him as he placed the ball and then backed away to wait for the referee to blow the whistle. As he stopped, he raised his fingertips to his lips and then touched them to his hip. She found another game with a penalty kick and saw him do the same. And another.

Leaning back in her desk chair, she pivoted to stare out into the garden while she pictured the sculpted planes and curved muscles of his body stretched out on her bed, marked only by scars and a single tattoo low on his hip. The shamrock with her initial at the center of it. She closed her eyes as the knowledge washed through her like the warmest, bluest Caribbean Sea chased by the bitterest, grayest salt ocean.

Just as she'd carried him with her, he'd carried her with him.

She deleted the folder with the videos in it before she jerked out of the chair, making it spin so hard it slammed into her desk and left a dent in the exotic Bolivian rosewood.

"Frankie." Gavin Miller's voice carried surprise as she walked up to the table in the Bellwether Club's bar.

Three men, all members, rose to their considerable heights, making her feel like an elderberry bush among redwoods. These were her three gamblers, who'd made a drunken bet on love three months before. They'd been strangers to each other then, but had been drawn into friendship by their wager.

Gavin, wearing his customary black sweater and jeans, was the bestselling author of the Julian Best novels, his super spy eclipsing James Bond as a cultural icon. Nathan Trainor, standing military straight in his custom-tailored navy suit, was the CEO and tech genius who'd founded Trainor Electronics, a Fortune 500 company. The golden-haired Luke Archer, his blue polo shirt and khakis stretched over a massive, but well-tuned athlete's frame, was the all-star franchise quarterback of the New York Empire, leading them to four Super Bowl wins thus far in his career.

"Gentlemen, I thought I'd buy you all a drink," she said. It was something of a joke at a club whose membership was limited to billionaires.

"We'd be honored," Luke said in his low Texas drawl. He pulled one of the massive, leather-upholstered club chairs to the table as though it weighed no more than a wicker basket.

As they settled back into their seats, her head bartender, Donal, brought another glass and a bottle of her usual drink, the same Redbreast 21 she'd served to Liam. That sent a ripple of pain through her but she stopped herself from wincing. She raised her glass. "*Sláinte.*"

Jesus, she couldn't stop herself from being Irish today.

The three men did a respectable job of echoing the Gaelic toast before they returned to the discussion of politics she'd interrupted. The exchange was lively because these were intelligent, worldly men, but she couldn't summon up enough interest to contribute to the debate.

Gavin, of course, noticed her distraction. "Frankie, I fear we're boring you."

"Not at all," she said, before sipping her whiskey. "I came to listen."

"And drink," Gavin said, as she refilled her glass for the second time. He was far too astute an observer. She should have avoided him.

"I can drink all of you under the table," she said. "It's in my DNA." There she went with the Irish thing again.

"Didn't I see you on the news with the new coach of the New York Challenge?" Nathan asked.

The remembered happiness of that day sent a jab of loss through her. "I know Liam from Dublin."

"I hear good things about him as a coach. I wish him luck." Luke smiled. "Wrong kind of football, but I won't hold that against him."

"He said the same thing about you," Frankie said.

"What did you think of Suicide Hill?" Nathan asked. "Was it as dangerous as it sounds?"

"Suicide Hill?" Gavin asked.

"That's what they call the sled run at Riverside Park and 91st," Nathan explained.

Gavin's gaze turned to Frankie. His gray-green eyes saw too much. "Frankie Hogan went sledding?"

"I was reliving my childhood in Ireland." A lie. She'd never once ridden a sled in Finglas.

"Ah, childhood. A dangerous time. No wonder you chose Suicide Hill to relive it on." Gavin's voice had turned sardonic.

"Let the lady enjoy her sledding," Luke said. "Not everyone has such a jaundiced view as you do."

"Because your youth was idyllic. All those picturesque longhorns and bouncy, blond cheerleaders," Gavin needled.

"I'm no more a poster child for a happy past than you are," the quarterback said.

Nathan swirled his Scotch in his cut crystal glass. "I suspect that our childhoods brought us to where we are, so maybe we shouldn't regret them. We certainly can't change them."

"I detect the hand of a woman in this sudden philosophical bent," Gavin said.

The CEO remained unruffled. "Chloe helped me make peace with my father. Now I can move forward."

"Can you?" Frankie asked, her voice sharp. "Can you leave your past behind?"

She felt the weight of their gazes.

Luke frowned as he considered her question. "You can learn to live with it. Not to let it make your decisions for you."

"How do you do that?" Frankie asked.

"Face it," Nathan said. "Understand how it formed you, so you can control your reactions now."

Gavin made an abrupt gesture with his hand. "Pretty words, but the past can be a slippery beast, slithering out of its cage and winding its coils around you like a boa constrictor."

He was a writer so it shouldn't surprise Frankie that he described her feelings so vividly.

"That's when you reach out." Luke's famous icy blue eyes warmed, and Frankie knew he was thinking of the woman he had declared his love for on national television. "The past is tough to handle without an outside perspective."

"And there you have it." Gavin lifted his glass high, his eyes flat with cynicism. "Love conquers all."

Frankie touched her glass to Gavin's before she swallowed the entire contents, hoping the burn of the liquor would counteract the chill that ran through her.

She loved Liam with every ounce of her being, but even he couldn't save her from her past.

CHAPTER TEN

"**M**s. Hogan, there's a gentleman here to see you." Vincent's voice came from behind her where she stood at the French doors in her office, feeling the cold seep through the plate glass as she stared at the swirling snow.

"On Christmas Eve?" She turned to catch a look of concern on her security chief's usually impassive face.

"He didn't want me to give his name, but it's Mr. Keller," Vincent said. "I'll escort him off the premises if you say the word."

"I'd like to see you try." Liam's voice came from the doorway, his tone pure gutter Finglas. He strode into the room, his long legs encased in charcoal gray trousers, his wide shoulders outlined by an open-necked shirt of the same deep blue as his eyes. A long, snow-dusted overcoat billowed around his legs.

She'd heard that a heart could leap, but she'd never felt it until now.

"We look down on brawling at the Bellwether Club." She kept her voice cool and controlled, despite the frantic dance of her pulse. "It's fine, Vincent."

As he left, her head of security threw Liam a look that would chill a lesser man's blood, but Liam shrugged it off as he focused on her.

"I'm sorry I left without saying good-bye to Owen," Frankie said, standing behind her desk.

"What about me?" Liam pulled a crumpled piece of paper from his pocket. "Did you think this was enough?" His voice had an edge like a razor blade.

She crossed her arms over her chest and looked away from the blaze of his blue eyes. "It was the best I could do at the time."

A flash of movement made her glance back at him to find he was circling around the desk. She stepped to the other side of her chair to keep something between them.

He stopped as he saw her withdrawal and ran a hand through the thick auburn waves of his hair in a gesture of frustration. "What made you run?"

"Ghosts." She shuddered as the memory clawed its way out of the dark corner where she'd shoved it.

"I'm your friend, even if you won't let me be anything more," he said. "I can help if you'll talk to me."

Despair dulled her voice. "The ghosts are here because of you."

She hated herself as soon as she saw the stricken look cloud the concern on his face. Her honesty was cruel but necessary.

"We'll fight them together then," he said.

She shook her head. "I lied to you about why I didn't let you know I was leaving Dublin twenty-three years ago. I wasn't afraid that you'd screw up your chances by leaving the training academy. I was afraid that if I saw you again, *I* wouldn't be able to go to America. You were my one weakness."

He shoved the chair aside and wrapped his fingers gently around her upper arms, his eyes alight with hope. "It's not a weakness to love someone."

She kept her arms crossed, even as the warmth of his touch infused the silk of her blouse.

He gave her the tiniest shake. "Give me your ghosts and I'll drag them out into the sunlight so they can never frighten you again." His gaze went a little wild as she stood silent. "Frankie, tell me!"

Maybe she owed him that. So she would let them rise up in her mind for his sake. "My sisters and brothers. We didn't have enough food because Da drank all his money and my mother was so broken she let him drink up hers too. All of us were always hungry." Their desperate voices echoed in her mind, begging her for something to eat. "I couldn't *do* anything. I felt powerless."

Liam's arms went around her and he pressed her against the solid comfort of his chest. But she couldn't yield to the temptation. She had to hold herself together as she told him her shameful secrets.

"I tried to get Ma to stand up to him, to keep at least the money *she* earned for the kids, but she just cried. That's when I knew it was all on me." Frankie could still remember the feeling that a heavy wet blanket had fallen over her, shrouding her in dark hopelessness. And helplessness. She'd been twelve at the time with no ability to earn the necessary money.

"Jaysus, Frankie, I had no idea it was that bad at your house. Why didn't you tell me?"

"What could you do? You went short of food too."

"I would have shared everything I had with you."

"That's why I didn't tell you. By the time I'd come to know you, I was earning enough so we always had something to eat, even after Da had taken his cut."

She felt him pull in a breath. "So you quit school and got the job at Balfour's to buy food. Not because the teachers had nothing more to teach you, like you always told me."

She tried to shrug out of his arms but he kept her close. "Now you know what made me run, Liam. I can't be around Owen. It sends me back to being that child filled with helplessness and rage. I panic." She tilted her head back to see pity in the softness of his mouth and eyes. She had to kill it. "I never want to be responsible for a child again."

Instead of backing away, he cradled her head with one gentle hand. "And who could blame you? I find it terrifying myself and I've only got the one, not to mention more than enough resources to buy him anything his heart desires. You had to raise seven children on a gofer's wages and you were just a child yourself. I've always thought you were an incredible woman, but this…this makes me feel awe."

"Don't you understand?" She slapped her palms against his chest, sensing the implacability of it. "I'm broken, just like my mother."

"Broken? Don't be daft. You're the strongest person I've ever met. All seven of your siblings are alive and well today. I can't say that about more than a quarter of our former neighbors. You saved your family." He moved one hand to cover hers where they rested on the fine cotton of his shirt. "You've bought your sisters and brothers houses, found them jobs, given them money. They've told me how good you've been to them."

"But I've never been to visit them. I've never invited them to visit me. I don't know any of their children." She swallowed, but her voice still came out as a harsh whisper. "And I can't bear to be around your son."

"I pushed too hard and fast. Because Christmas was coming and I wanted—" He closed his eyes for a moment, the angles of his face taut with longing. "I wanted the three of us to be together, like a family." He shook his head. "But that was my dream, not yours. Forgive me. I won't force it again."

His understanding brought a burn of tears to her eyes. "You need to be with Owen."

"Today, I need to be with you. It's Christmas Eve, Frankie. The night of miracles. We can make ours happen."

She kept her hands wedged between them as she felt a yearning to believe a miracle was possible. "I don't doubt your love. Or mine. But we both love a memory. We've walked different paths for so many years. We're not the same people."

"That's where you're wrong. We've become the people we plotted and planned and worked our arses off to be. I didn't love just you. I loved the person you would be."

All her defenses reared up in a last-ditch effort to keep her in her lonely, safe cocoon. She thought of the moment in Yankee Stadium when she'd seen him as her equal for the first time. "But we're different together. The dynamic has changed."

He smiled down at her, the heat of desire turning his eyes an intense sapphire. "And I'm liking it."

She was lost, overwhelmed by the feel of his body against hers, by the wanting in his eyes, by his answers for every one of her objections. No, she was overwhelmed by the power of the love that had been forged in the despair and stink of the slums, had endured through their single-minded climbs to the top, and had brought them back together now.

One deep fear held her in its grip. "What if I can never stand to be near Owen?"

She saw the pain in his eyes, but also the willingness to accept it for her sake. "Owen won't be a child forever." Then he smiled in a way that she felt to the marrow of her bones. "But I believe you can conquer anything you set your mind to, *á stor*."

"It's a big risk."

"And when did a risk ever stop either one of us? Consider it a Christmas gamble. The chance of a lifetime."

The warmth of his belief soaked into every dark corner of her soul.

His eyes burned as blue as a blowtorch. "Now I intend to give you a kiss that will wipe out all your doubts. And I came prepared." He rummaged in his coat pocket and pulled out a single sprig of mistletoe tied with a tiny red bow. "Just in case you needed more persuading."

Taking the mistletoe from his grasp, she held it high as she slipped her other hand around the back of his neck to pull him down to meet her mouth.

She let all the love she'd fought against so long and so hard roar through her as she kissed him, the Liam of her past, present, and future.

EPILOGUE

Ten Months Later

Frankie walked back into Nathan and Chloe's wedding reception to find Liam leaning against the wall, waiting for her. He looked so gloriously sexy in his cream-colored linen suit that she wanted to take him back to the jet and strip his clothes right off. But she couldn't leave the wedding before the bride and groom did.

So she contented herself with sliding her arm under his jacket to trace her fingers up his spine while she whispered what she wanted to do when the reception ended.

His blue eyes turned hot as he bent to murmur beside her ear, "You read my mind, *a stór.*" He held out his hand and twined his fingers with hers as soon as she took it. "Let's take a walk away from the crowd."

He led her out a side door into the soft caress of the autumn air in North Carolina.

"Nathan says this is one of the three days it's bearable to be outdoors at Camp Lejeune," Frankie said, as they strolled across the grass toward the bank of the New River. The scent of brackish water—part sea, part earth—filled her nostrils.

"Did your three gamblers burn their wagers?" Liam asked as they stopped to take in the view of water and trees.

"All ashes now. I left them toasting their new wives in champagne." Nathan had been the first of the three men to get engaged—thus winning his portion of the bet—but the last to get married, so his wedding had been chosen for the ceremonial burning of the men's written forfeits, marking the successful completion of their wager of hearts. For a while, Frankie had been worried that Gavin Miller would fail, but even the darkly cynical writer had found a soulmate. "I owe them all a debt of gratitude," she said. "They knew something important was missing from their lives, something that made them desperate enough to bet on love. If I hadn't seen that, I might not have been as willing to take the risk with you."

"And that is the perfect introduction to why I lured you out here alone," Liam said, holding both her hands in his. He took a deep breath and locked his deep blue gaze on her face. "These last ten months have been the best of my life. Seeing you and Owen together—" She watched the muscles of his throat work as he swallowed against some powerful emotion. "—has brought me a joy beyond all my dreams."

After Frankie's panic attack at Paddy's Pub, Liam had backed off and let Frankie come to know Owen at her own pace. They'd started with a trip to the Museum of Natural History, neutral territory with no triggers. Once she and Owen got on the subject of chemistry, their relationship progressed smoothly.

Now Owen regularly visited with her in the Bellwether Club's kitchen to concoct new flavors of chocolate and other more volatile chemical combinations. The chef viewed their presence with trepidation, but Frankie loved seeing what experiments the boy's agile mind created, even if they occasionally exploded.

Frankie squeezed Liam's hands. "You were right...Owen and I are kindred spirits." She loved to watch Liam with his son too. The bond between the two of them had grown strong now that Liam spent so much time with Owen. He was one lucky kid.

Liam's grip tightened. "So there is no reason why we shouldn't officially become a family." With all the graceful control of a well-conditioned athlete, he sank onto one knee, his face tilted up to hers. "I remember the day we met. My soccer ball was about to be mashed by a car, when you darted into the street and kicked it back to me. I fell in love with you in that moment."

Frankie's heart was trying to pound its way out of her chest to say "yes", but she wasn't going to let him off that easily. "That was gratitude, not love, ye right eejit. I'd saved your most precious possession."

"I should have known you'd ruin my heartfelt speech," he said, amusement and exasperation in his eyes. "Have you no romance in your soul at all?"

"I'm an American. We like to get to the point."

"All right then." All the amusement left his expression and he took another deep breath. "Will you do me the honor of marrying me?"

Her heart seemed to beat in her throat, so it was hard to speak. "Yes."

There was a moment of silence before he said, "That's all? Just *yes*?"

"Did I not wake up in your bed this morning and tell you that I loved you and then proceed to demonstrate just how much? Did I not tell you ten minutes ago that I wanted to go back to the jet, strip naked, and make love for the entire flight back to New York?" She softened her voice. "Do I need to tell you again that I adore you with everything in me?"

"I never tire of hearing it."

"Stand up, and I'll show you."

"I'm not finished." He released her hands and reached into his coat pocket, pulling out a black velvet box. He flipped the lid open and drew out a ring, holding out his hand for hers. "It's an emerald, Frankie," he said as he slid it on, the brush of his long fingers sending a shiver of warmth up her arm. "Because no matter how bad it was, Ireland was where we started. Even more important, Ireland is where I fell irrevocably in love with you."

She brushed her fingertips down his cheek, marveling at the way the boy had changed—and not changed—into the man. Wondering how she had inspired the kind of love that burned bright and true through the years of separation. Knowing that she had carried him in her heart through all that time too.

"The emerald is exactly right," she said, as the deep green gem glowed in a slant of sunlight. "I've learned to be proud of where I came from because it brought me you."

He rose in the same way he'd knelt…with perfect efficiency in every muscle. It gave her pleasure simply to watch him move.

"I tried to guess how I'd feel at this moment," he said, cradling her face in his big hands. "But I had no idea that I would feel not just joy, but peace. Finglas is where I lived but you were always my home. And now I'm where I belong…with you."

He touched his lips to hers with such tenderness that tears brimmed in her eyes, spilling over as her eyelids closed to savor the feel of his body against hers. His soft, firm mouth grazed the wet streaks on her cheeks.

"Don't cry, *a stór,*" he murmured against her skin, his breath a caress. "We've earned our happiness."

"You've made me feel again, so you'll have to take the tears as part of that." She opened her eyes and ran her fingers through the gleaming waves of his auburn hair, touching the glint of silver at his temple. "Let's get married as soon as we get back to New York. I know a judge or two."

"Oh, no, my lovely jackeen. We're getting married in St. Patrick's Cathedral. And you're going to invite all your billionaire friends. I want the world to know that you're mine at long last."

She opened her mouth to argue, but saw the steel in his eyes. She felt the glow of satisfaction at his desire to claim her publicly. "I'm not so well acquainted with the archbishop."

"Ah, but I am. He's a soccer fan."

Frankie laughed. Liam had fulfilled his prophecy of building a soccer team that galvanized New York City. The upstart Challenge had clinched a spot in the playoffs the week before, and the city was buzzing with excitement. "You'd better win the MLS Cup then."

The steel was still there when he said, "I intend to."

The raw determination in his voice sent a streak of heat flashing through her. She wove her fingers into the hair at the nape of his neck and pulled him down for a searing kiss, then leaned back against his arms. It seemed a good time to discuss the idea she'd been considering. "Speaking of soccer—"

"Soccer? What's soccer?" His gaze scorched over her as he started to pull her close again.

She wedged her arms between them. "Good. I've got you in the right frame of mind."

"You mean you've blown my mind to bits." He loosened his hold with a sigh of resignation.

"You remember how lonely you were when you went away to the training academy and lived in the dormitory?"

"I try not to." But he nodded.

"I was thinking that we might bring some of the talented Irish kids from Finglas and similar neighborhoods over here to train. Except we'll have them live with us, now that you're making an honest woman of me. That way they'll have a family environment, even though they're far from home."

Liam went still against her for a long moment before his words seemed to burst from him. "Jaysus, Joseph, and Mary, you can still surprise me." He picked her up like she was a mere girl and spun around in a circle before he gave her a smacking kiss on the lips. "I should know that it's all or nothing with you. You took to Owen, so now you want a whole herd of kids. I love you for it."

"It still hurts me that I can't give you children," she said, the truth of it making her stomach clench. "But I'm learning to believe that you can live with that."

"You're not doing this just to make me happy, are you?" Liam frowned, even as he continued to hold her up against him, her feet dangling.

"I would, if I thought that's what you needed, but no. I love having Owen with us. He fills the place with life and energy. I want more of that."

His smile returned. "We'll buy a big house so you can have as much energy as you can stand."

"It will cut into our sex life," she said. "All those kids around all the time."

"Not a chance." He let her slide down the front of his hard, muscular body with exquisite slowness until her feet were back on the ground. "Our new house will have a master suite that's miles away from the kids' rooms."

"But what about sex on the kitchen counter?" She thought of that particular location with great fondness.

"I'll have a counter built in the bedroom. With a height adjustment so it will be even more... versatile." His voice was a rumbling croon as he nuzzled behind her ear, while a tingle of sensation traveled down her neck, through her breasts, to settle between her legs.

"And we can always take the limo out if we need more privacy," she said, her voice a rasp at the memories of their bare skin against black leather seats.

"Not to mention a private terrace." He pulled back which allowed her to see the intensity of his eyes. "Because I'll need to make love to you there every time it snows."

She knew her eyes mirrored his as she remembered the profound connection of their first time together, a connection that had deepened every day since. "In that case, I'll be hoping for an ice age."

ACKNOWLEDGMENTS

This novella was a work of pure pleasure, meant as a gift to all my wonderful readers who asked to spend more time in my Wager of Hearts world. I have always wanted to write an older heroine and a hero who is younger than she is. Frankie was there at the Bellwether Club, just waiting for Liam to upend her carefully ordered world with his undying passion.

However, a book written for fun requires all the same research and polishing as any other story. I wouldn't give my loyal readers any less. Which means that I needed all the same help from a great team of experts. A huge thank you to:

My Handsome Husband, Jeff, who is not a soccer aficionado but dug into the Internet to educate me on the world of European "football". Being a sports enthusiast, he could read between the lines when I got lost in the jargon. He did double duty as my meticulous proofreader too.

Lisa Verge Higgins, my brilliant critique partner, who happens to be a genius at developmental editing, as well as writing pithy, enticing book description blurbs.

Ashley Martin at Twin Tweaks Editing, who combed through this story with precision and care to make sure my sentences were clear, and my capitals, hyphens, and commas were all in the right places. Any mistakes I made in this acknowledgement are all mine.

Rogenna Brewer, my incredible cover designer, who found the perfect Liam and put the perfect Christmas brownstone behind him *on the first try!* Is she a mind reader or just a terrific artist? Or possibly both?

My critique partners, Miriam Allenson, the aforementioned Lisa Verge Higgins, and Jennifer Wilck, who offer great insight, excellent suggestions, and tough love, as well as the warmest support any writer could ask for.

Cathy Genna, my delightful assistant, who arranged and rearranged title options until we found just the right combination of words. She knows readers so well.

And always, Jeff, Rebecca, and Loukas, who applaud my successes, commiserate with my disappointments, and show me over and over again how powerful love is.

ABOUT THE AUTHOR

Nancy Herkness is the author of the award-winning Wager of Hearts and Whisper Horse series, published by Montlake Romance, as well as several other contemporary romance novels. She is a two-time nominee for the Romance Writers of America's RITA® award.

Nancy is a member of Romance Writers of America, New Jersey Romance Writers, and Novelists, Inc. She has received many honors for her work, including the Book Buyers Best Top Pick, the New England Readers' Choice award, and the National Excellence in Romance Fiction award. She graduated from Princeton University with a degree in English literature and creative writing.

A native of West Virginia, Nancy now lives in suburban New Jersey with her husband, two mismatched dogs, and an elderly cat.

For more information about Nancy and her books, visit her website: www.NancyHerkness.com. You can also find her on Facebook and Pinterest.

Made in the USA
Middletown, DE
30 July 2018